The Battle
for
Q'Door Hold

G M McRae

The Battle

for

Q'Door Hold

Best wishes!
G. M. McRae

G M McRae

Dedication

I DEDICATE THIS BOOK TO MY FAMILY.

Acknowledgements

This book survived our moving, having more children, and losing part of the manuscript. Yet, here it is, thanks to the following wonderful people I am blessed to have in my life: my husband, Philip, who encouraged me when I needed it most and who didn't fuss when I sat in my chair for hours on end writing; my granddaughter, Elizabeth, who listened to the first tentative chapters - the light in her eyes gave me the courage to go on; my son Phil, who read the first very rough draft and thought it was awesome, even then; my son Pat and daughter Kate who, though away in college, encouraged me along the way. I also want to thank Jennifer and Chris Fore, who read the fourth draft, and gave me valuable input. Their suggestions helped me smooth out the rough spots.

I want to thank my sister-by-choice Delores Alston for loving me anyway, even when I couldn't call or visit like I wanted to during the writing of this book.

Thanks also go to my friend Sarah Shipman, whose insights helped me put the finishing touches on this effort.

Thanks most of all to God who gave me the ability to write this story.

Table of Contents

He leaned against a skiabar tree, shadows hiding his watching. How long would he have before he was summoned again? Brushing the remnants of his meal from his tunic, the Rider turned back to his world. 'How odd,' he thought, 'to live between times, among the infinity of the universe. And for what?' He sighed. His young son slid clumsily from the tree across the quad. He'd been trying desperately to ride as his father did, effortlessly and undetected. 'Ah well. He's still young.' He strode over and picked up the giggling boy, tossing him onto his shoulders. They disappeared into the nothingness that took them home.

———— ⌘ ————

The Winds of Change

The seventh world of the Reglon Empire was in trouble - again. Creedor had been annexed when the Supreme Commander of the Empire Fleet overthrew their aging leader, The Right Reverend Elder Horatio Borm. The coup had been well executed and surprisingly easy for Jarlod, who used his position to accomplish the deed. Though he had great power, Jarlod wanted more. He had broken bread with the Elder, laughed at his simple jokes, all the while waiting for the right time to strike. His patience paid off when Elder Borm became ill. Jarlod had shown no mercy. He had no intention of letting the old man interfere with his rise to power. Jarlod, now the self-declared Emperor, began by taking all surrounding worlds that might be of use to him. Creedor, the first to be conquered was most important because it was the source of almost all the trizactl in the galaxy; only trace amounts had been found elsewhere. Jarlod needed this mineral to power the massive weapons his military engineers had designed. But that wasn't the only reason he needed to control this planet. Jarlod was evil, but not stupid. He knew that his military force would need food, and Creedor was a leader in food production. While the majority of Creedor's surface was covered with a fine, brown sand, there were underground rivers that in places rose close to the surface producing valleys so lush and green that farming flourished.

There were also several large tredon herds being raised for commercial use on the windswept plateaus. Tredons were beasts almost impervious to the elements. They thrived on desert vegetation, soaking up the heat from the sun-baked sand. Their hides sold at a premium to clothing manufacturers when the tredon had lived on the plateaus at least four seasons. It took that long for the sun to bake and the sand to etch the unusual patterns that were so prized among the leather wrights. But the hides reached their greatest value when harvested after the tredons' tenth season; by then they were tempered like the finest metal making them virtually impenetrable. Paradoxically, tredon meat was the most inexpensive of any to be had in the Empire. It was always tender and there was plenty of it because few were selected at birth for the hide herds. The rest were shipped to farms in the valleys to be raised for meat or placed in the dairy stock. Almost all of the tredon could be used for something, so there was very little waste, an attribute that Jarlod failed to comprehend, but the tredon farmers prized.

Now Creedor, having survived eons of ecological abuse and enemy invasions, was once again under assault. This time the enemy was a mysterious disease discovered by the crew of a supply ship on a routine run. When the Emperor got wind of it, he decided to take a closer look at Creedor and sent scouts to assess the situation. The report was grim: The disease was killing citizens by the hundreds, throwing the populace into a state of utter chaos. It wasn't until Commander Michael Camdus was assigned to Creedor that a much more insidious threat was discovered.

Out of the Frying Pan

The southern moon was riding high above the Creedorian Mountains. Fiery wind whipped the dark sand across the walking yard of the Tonlin's home. Mara Tonlin busied herself in the kitchen as she waited for her husband Ramar to return from taking care of the animals. The howling outside sent a chill through her fragile spirit. It was dangerous to be out when the southern moon was full, especially now that the epidemic was ravaging their village. Many of the afflicted had gone mad and spent their incredible fury on anything or anyone they came upon. Those with the disease could find no peace. Their lives became progressively more horrific until the last throes of the sickness. The afflicted were often so disfigured that their own families couldn't recognize them. When the illness finally ran its course, the victims crumpled where they stood and died the slow, agonizing death that made this unknown ailment so feared.

The back door slammed into the wall as Ramar hurried in, swirls of dust with him. Mara raced to secure the door as he collapsed at the table.

"Mara, I don't know how much longer we can hold out here," Ramar finally admitted. "If the epidemic doesn't get us, we may well starve. The herd has wandered so far away from the ranch that I don't think I can round them up until after demon wind season is over. And the rest of the livestock are beginning to weaken for lack of feed. I couldn't get any milk from either tredon cow. And the bull looked yellow-eyed and his breathing was raspy like your mare before she died last week." Mara winced at the mention of her prized mare, Abalon. Her father had given the horse to Mara when she was a teenager. Wherever Mara had gone, Abalon had been brought along, too. Even so, losing Abalon was the smallest of their losses. Mara had shed too many tears already. Now she needed to look after Ramar.

Mara sat down beside him and leaned her head on his shoulder; the grit on his shirt stuck to her cheek. How could she comfort him when she felt no comfort herself? Ramar had been her rock, her source of strength since they lost their only child to the disease. Watching their tiny daughter change from a beautiful happy toddler into a sallow, wizened animal that growled and bit had been sheer agony for them both. Ram had been forced to administer a tranquilizer to calm her. To get close enough, he had put on his old battle uniform for protection. Ram had cradled Astril in his arms as she fell into a deep sleep; she had regained consciousness only once before she died.

With Astril gone, Mara felt as if her heart had been ripped from her chest, leaving a gaping hole in her soul. She had managed to pull herself together, but there were days her entire being was sucked into that abyss, leaving no room for even the thought that she might feel joy again. And Mara knew that Ram's misery now was a reflection of the pain that he felt after losing his baby girl. Astril had been the bright spot in his life and he had doted on her, as many a father before him had doted on an only daughter. Mara's own grief had been spent holding onto Ram as she wept herself to sleep each night for what felt like forever. He'd had no time to grieve, for Mara had needed him to be strong.

But now, with the onset of the demon winds and the lack of food on top of the epidemic, it seemed that Ramar just could not hold up anymore. Every time Mara was tempted to break into the store of emergency food, Ram stopped her with, "Not yet, Mara." All of these worries seemed to distance Ram even further from her. To Mara, it was as if the very heart and life had abandoned Ram and that was almost more than she could bear. She placed her arms around his neck and stroked his thick black hair, a sprinkle of reddish brown sand salting the table. Ram was the bravest, kindest man Mara had ever known. When they first met, his vivid blue eyes seemed to sparkle from his rugged tanned face. When he smiled at her, she felt happy. But now there was no sparkle in his eyes, no smile on his face. He seemed to have aged twenty years in less than one. He never wanted to just sit with her, talking or just being. He used to notice her corn silk hair, teasing that she must have had elven ancestors. Though they lived in the same house, they definitely lived in separate hearts. 'How long can we survive like this? There must be something we can do. Somewhere, somehow, someone has got to help us,' she thought, her spirit heavy with despair. Yet, even in this depth of sorrow, her ardent prayer for help ran through her mind one more time.

"Ram, come on, you need to get some rest. I'll run your bath so you can clean up and then turn in. There's nothing else you can do this evening anyway." Ramar looked at Mara with lifeless eyes. He hoisted himself up from the chair. Sand was embedded in his skin, hair, and clothes. His anger was so great that he felt like shouting in God's face, but his will was gone. Totally frustrated, he followed Mara to their bathroom where he mechanically undressed. The warmth of the bath water seeped into his body, but misery stubbornly clung to his spirit. Mara quietly closed the door as she left. She was drawn as always to the window that faced the walking yard. The endless patterns of shifting sand fascinated her, though the demon wind season was one to be feared during the best of times. And now . . . .

Mara's thoughts were interrupted by the sudden realization that the roar of the wind had changed. It sounded almost as if a ship were landing. But that couldn't be. No one would be foolish enough to try to land on Creedor during demon wind season. Those winds could toss a ship as easily as tossing a toy, destroying it and everyone on board. Yet, as she peered out into the growing darkness, she thought she saw something on the horizon. It couldn't be. Could it?

"Ramar! Come here. Hurry! I think something is happening outside; and I don't know, but I think we may have company. Maybe it's someone from the Empire coming to help us." Ram didn't answer, so she called again, louder this time, "Ramar, Ramar!"

Ram had heard her, but her words had taken a moment to register. He sprang from the tub, swiftly drying and donning a clean under-form. "Mara, get away from that window!" Ram shouted as he sped to the living room, deftly covering his too lean, yet still strong body with his battle uniform as he ran.

With a final snap of his boot strap, he reached Mara and shouted, "Put out the lights. It could be one of them. Mara, we've got to keep our wits about us if we're going to survive. You know if they find us, they'll take us captive." Ramar shook Mara, who still stood peering into the growing gloom.

"Mara, help me secure the house." Back to reality, Mara swiftly made sure windows and shutters were locked down tight.

"Now go to your station and stay there until I come for you." Mara realized how careless she had been and raced to the secret room behind the panel in the closet of their bedroom. She felt for the light switch on the wall. The room was instantly bathed in a pale bluish gray light. Her heart was pounding so loudly she was afraid whoever was outside would hear it and find her. She began taking deep, slow, steady breaths to calm herself. 'Ramar, please be careful,' she whispered into the night, though she knew he could not hear her. The two-foot thick wall that Ram had designed and built was soundproof. Thankfully, Ram also had made sure the room was ventilated, with a filtration system to allow only fresh air without the stifling sand. During demon wind season, she had to remember to push the button marked "Purge" at least twice a day to keep the filter clean. Ram had located a natural spring in the rock wall, a perfect source of cool, fresh water. He had long ago stored their meager survival supplies under the handmade cot. A tiny water closet had been hewn into the far end of the space and plumbed to run well away from their home. Ram had been determined to provide for the essentials. She remembered the excitement and pride when he had finished their secret room. Her memories of their celebration at his triumph usually made her smile. But now, Mara could only pray that he would come for her soon. She knelt beside the cot, head bowed, and opened her heart to God.

Doctor for Hire

On Ashtar, Slogar had been a struggling student of medical history, until genetic engineering finally erased major diseases. He had always been more of a bookworm than a doer, so studying medical history had seemed the path for him. Medicine, as in becoming a doctor, would have required sure-enough work and dedication, two things Slogar had no interest in. In short order after the big declaration that the Empire was now without disease, the Emperor discontinued all medical programs, including classes in its history. Physicians were rounded up and sent into new professions. Those who resisted were not heard from again. Lazy though he was, this really hacked Slogar. He could not accept the premise that there would never again be a need for physicians because he could not believe that tampering with genetics wouldn't create other problems – and diseases – in the long run.

Slogar left Ashtar and went to Andalla for some years, where he tried quietly to continue his study of ancient medicine, without being noticed. Yet he was noticed, and not favorably. The Andallans were somewhat low-brow, to borrow an antiquated term. The majority of them were quite content to live in mediocrity, never challenging edicts sent out by the Emperor no matter how ludicrous. Jarlod's narcissistic nature framed his leadership style – persecute and bully to get what he wanted. He disrespected everyone around him, including his Council of Elders to whom he owed so much. Without the support of three or four key members, his coup would have failed. Now Jarlod deceived and outright lied to all of them as he sank deeper into his own delusions. But the Andallans smiled, complacently believing their Emperor was God, or a very good facsimile. Slogar had on more than one occasion taken a pounding for daring to disagree with something the Emperor had said or done. And this business of no doctors, well, Slogar was just plain furious.

The angrier he became, the greater Slogar's thirst for knowledge grew. His complacency was replaced by a fire. He felt a sense of urgency that he couldn't explain, but he knew he had not only to learn about the history of medicine, but also to master the techniques involved in treating the sick. Living on Andalla made this goal very hard to attain as he had to watch out for the Emperor's spies and for the Andallans who thought it their duty to trounce anyone who disagreed with the Emperor. Slogar was forced to take risks in gaining the forbidden knowledge of medicine. Sneaking into old abandoned libraries under the cloak of night gave up little information that he didn't already have. But as he continued his search, he began to wonder what had happened to the physicians who practiced before the ban but were never heard of again. There was a legend of one who used to live on Andalla. He searched carefully for information to lead him to this physician, hoping that she was still alive. While everyone on Andalla had heard of the Elder Woman who lived a solitary life away from civilization, few knew that she had been a doctor. Most people thought she was an oracle, others thought she was just a crazy old lady. Slogar didn't know which she one she was, but he knew he had to find out.

In one of his frequent nightly forays, Slogar entered one of the less used museums. In a dust laden room at the back, he found a small archive of articles from an old medical journal. In it he found one that spoke of this very lady as having been not only a physician but also a researcher until she was "purified." Slogar was not sure what that meant exactly, and the article didn't spell it out, but he was pretty sure that it had been a messy business. He wondered if she survived; and if she did survive, could she possibly have her right mind after this "purification"?

With these questions nagging him more and more incessantly, he realized he no longer could take not knowing. So he set out to find the Elder Woman of Silden across Andalla's sparsely populated plains. After several days of slow travel over the bleak terrain, he came upon a lonely farm. He had been walking for some time that day and decided to take a rest inside the old shanty house that sat about a hundred yards off the rutted road, ankle deep in very warm sand. He navigated through the tangle of weeds that littered the path to the house. His robe was covered with what the ancients would have called 'beggar lice,' though they were really just prickly seeds. Carefully, he navigated his bulk up the rickety steps onto the uneven porch. There was a wooden chair on the porch, but its legs were so rotted it sat at a forty-five degree angle. He thought maybe the inside would prove to be more solid, so he entered the door, which hung raggedly from its hinges.

At first all he saw were a dust-laden wooden table and chairs, and a straw bed on the floor near a hearth that looked as if it had been barren of heat for many seasons. He gingerly, well as gingerly as he was able, made his way to the hearth. A round of tree trunk about two and a half feet high sat beside the hearth. He carefully lowered himself onto it and emptied the sand from his shoes. Slogar reckoned he was close to the Elder Woman's home, so he could afford to stop for the evening. After resting a bit, he got up and began to investigate the small shelter. He was pleasantly surprised to find two tredon oil lamps and a striker. He lit one of them and set it on the table in the center of the room. He turned up the wick to cast a brighter light. The pair of glowing eyes among a pile of rags on the straw mat startled him. He jumped back, shaking the floor so violently that one of the chairs fell over. 'Okay. Now what?' He'd been so careful to carry all that he needed to continue his studies that he didn't even think about a weapon. Well, he still had his wits. The eyes glowed yellow.

Taking a deep breath, Slogar said, "Umm, ah, hello. Uh, I, ah, just thought I'd stop for a minute to rest. So um now I have and I'll just be on my way." The pile of rags rose so fast from the floor that Slogar had no time to escape. Before his eyes, the dirty old rags turned into fine, emerald green robes and the yellow eyes became a translucent, pale blue. He stood speechless.

"So, Simon Slogar, you finally found me. I have waited many months for this day." Slogar stammered, "You know me? How? But I ...." The stately woman who now stood before him waved him to silence.

"I am Elder Woman Seelah. Your search for me was by my design. There are things we must discuss and things I must teach you if you are to fulfill your destiny."

Slogar tended to babble when scared, so he began, "My destiny? I don't have a destiny, other than to do my best to dodge the Emperor's henchmen. I'm just a self-taught student of ancient medicine; not very well taught at that. And my curiosity has caused more trouble than you can know, yet I have not been able to curb it. So, I've had to move from place to place, planet to planet to keep from becoming a guest on Helgrad. But, how did you...? I mean, what ARE you talking about? I came looking for you because *I* want to ask *you* about some of the ancient pox remedies. Why would you think you brought me here?" He was a little indignant that this woman, elder or not, thought she could control him, could MAKE him do something without his knowing it.

Seelah laughed softly, clearly trying not to offend, but unable to contain herself. 'Poor man,' she thought, 'how many have thought their behavior was purely their choice.'

"Simon. May I call you 'Simon'?" He nodded; there was something about this woman that put him at ease once the initial shock wore off. "Simon, I have willed you here because the whole Empire is in danger. There is still time to prepare, but only you are advanced enough to take the knowledge I will give you and use it with the skills and knowledge you already have to devise a solution."

Slogar looked at Seelah for a moment before he spoke. "Why don't you solve the problem yourself, whatever it is? I mean, after all, you did will me here, right? If you can do that, surely you can figure out how to overcome any problem." Seeing the look on Seelah's face, he quickly added, "No disrespect intended, Elder Woman."

Seelah sighed. She had expected this. "I am the Elder Woman *of Silden*. If I leave these plains, I lose my most powerful abilities, my gifts, if you will. I had to bring you here to take on this task. Though you see yourself as, well, a lost cause, I do not. I know that the intellectual gifts God has given you are not bound to any place. With your help, we can overcome the threat. Will you stay with me awhile? I promise you that much of the knowledge you have so futilely sought will be made known to you. Are you willing?"

"Do I have to give you my answer right now?" Slogar deeply regretted his decision to take a rest in this cottage. No, he regretted setting out in the first place.

The Elder Woman responded evenly, "I'm afraid so, Simon; we have no time to spare."

Slogar was overcome by an intense craving for ale. He reached into his pack, desperately looking through the bottles until he found one that wasn't empty, but was awfully close. 'Oh, great,' he thought, 'just my luck.' But he lifted his head and gave Seelah the only viable answer, "All right. I'll stay, but you need to understand my limitations."

Seelah looked at him as a mother looks at her petulant child. "Yes, Simon, I am aware of your limitations; I am also aware that most of them are of your own making. We will work on eliminating them as we go." She reached out and took the pack from him, taking the bottles one by one and placing them on the table. "You won't need these anymore." Without any more questions, Simon Slogar became a reluctant student of Elder Woman of Silden, far away from civilization on the desolate plains of Andalla.

The Elder Woman's
Secret Laboratory

Seelah walked to the hearth and with her left hand touched the dusty mantle. "Take my hand." Slogar looked tentatively at the extended right hand, wondering what he was getting into. In a rare moment of swift decision, he took the hand. The room as he knew it faded away. He had the distinct feeling of free falling through a fog. When he could catch his breath again, he saw that he and the Elder Woman were standing in a pristine, blindingly white room. Bottles and vials glinted under the bright light whose source he could not determine. The air bore an acrid smell so sharp that Slogar's eyes began to water.

"My eyes! Seelah, what is happening to my eyes?" The Elder Woman placed a cool hand over Slogar's eyes. He felt instant relief.

"Disinfectant. You'll get used to it." Slogar wondered what else he'd have to get used to, but he was in it now and saw no way out. She gave him a small jar of the cooling salve she had just used to calm his burning eyes.

"Use this until your eyes adjust to the stringent effects of the disinfectant. I keep this room germ free. As we fell, we passed through a mist that killed any bacteria we may have picked up on the surface."

"The surface? So that means we're underground?" Seelah nodded, changing the lighting to a setting that would be kinder to the doctor's eyes.

"We need to get started, but first let me show you to your room so you can settle in." She led him through a passageway that he had not noticed before. All along the way were doors, each bearing a symbol that was totally unknown to Slogar. At last they stopped before a door. Slogar was surprised to see his own name there. Seelah opened the door and invited him to enter. This room was an exact replica of the room he had occupied at his home on Ashtar.

"I hope you are pleased, Simon." At a loss for words, he could only blink at her. This was beyond anything he could comprehend. How could she have known? He walked over to his bureau and opened the top drawer, half expecting to find the clothes he had worn all those years ago. He was relieved to find cloaks and uniforms that were distinctly more practical as his girth had more than doubled.

"Simon, we'll have dinner at six. I'll send Elani to escort you to the dining chamber." Seelah left Simon still clearly confused. He took some time to put his things away, and then found a bath chamber adjacent to a very large closet. It had been a long time since he had actually disrobed and bathed, but he felt the need to do so in this pristine facility. He stepped into the ample shower stall and was instantly soaked with jets of foam spraying him from all directions. After a few minutes of this, the foam was replaced by clear water. The disinfectant smell that had permeated his senses ever since he got here was replaced by a fresh scent that reminded him of a sunshine drenched meadow that he had played in as a child on Ashtar. The water stopped and Slogar stepped out into a small alcove just to the left of the bath. There he found a large warm towel which he gratefully clutched to him as he walked back into his room to dress. A knock at the door some time later let him know that it was time for dinner.

Elani was a tall, thin woman of indeterminate age and ancestry. Her soft voice had a soothing quality to it that Slogar found immensely appealing. "Dr. Slogar, please come with me."

"Gladly, my dear," Slogar said as he offered Elani his arm. Not really understanding this strange custom, she smiled and preceded him to the lift. After a brief moment the lift paused, then opened its doors onto yet another chamber. This one was softly lit and filled with the smell of roasted meat and savory spices. His mouth began to water. The Elder Woman was standing by a huge brick hearth. She seemed lost in thought, so he quietly followed Elani to a sturdy sofa. Elani did not speak, but nodded her farewell and quietly glided from the chamber. Slogar waited for Seelah to join him. After a bit, she turned and smiled at him.

"Good evening, Simon. Are you hungry? Elani has prepared a wonderful roast for us with pickled eggs and some of the greens she grew in the hydro garden." Slogar was very hungry and indicated this by rising and offering her his arm to escort her to the table, which stood in an alcove to the rear of the sitting area. Seelah gracefully laid her hand upon his arm. It had been quite a long time since a gentleman had offered her his arm. Though he was not as old as she, he did observe the old rules of courtesy that she found pleasing. After seating her at one end of the wooden table, he seated himself at the other. The meal before him was more a feast than anything else. He placed his napkin in his lap and took up his fork and knife.

"Simon, would you please ask the blessing for the meal?" Slogar had not returned thanks for a meal since he was a child, but he felt he had to do as Seelah asked.

"God is great, God is good. Let us thank him for this food. Amen." Seelah smiled. She knew a child's prayer when she heard one, but at least somewhere in his childhood he had been exposed to faith in something greater than himself. So maybe he wasn't hopeless in that regard either. Slogar looked up, a sheepish smile on his face.

After they had eaten in silence for a while, he asked, "How long have you lived here, Seelah?"

The Elder Woman finished the morsel in her mouth before answering. "I've been here since my purification was deemed a success, about twenty years ago. The Emperor's henchmen loaded me and seventeen others into a podtrans and then dumped us out on the edge of the plain without even a bottle of water or crust of bread. Some went into hysterics and ran after them only to be vaporized right in front of us. The rest of us, twelve there were, huddled among the tumblers and scroots that grow wild along the roadsides. As soon as they left, we struck out across the arid plains, with no one talking, no one leading, just walking. Fairly soon I realized that most of them would not make it because they now had the minds of small children. They followed us, but often strayed to look at a pretty flower or strange design in the sand. Only three of us had managed to survive purification without any real damage to our minds. And we did that only by pretending to be like the others."

Slogar listened to Seelah's story as he reached for more bread and meat. The wine, a very light red was nowhere near as strong as he would have liked, but it went well with the meal. He refilled his glass. Seelah drank the last of her wine and delicately wiped her mouth with her linen napkin. She sat quietly. Slogar wanted to hear more, but felt it best to wait for her to pick up the story thread again. He was disappointed when she said, "Well, I think that's enough for now. I'm going to retire for the evening. Please feel free to stay up as long as you like, but I must caution you to stay in this wing. And do not try to return to the surface." Slogar said nothing, but was thinking, 'I'd rather eat scroots than go back through that hateful mist.'

He made himself focus on what Seelah was saying. "Jarlod's men patrol this area frequently; I think it's best they not know of this place. I have no desire to be captured again. Once in a lifetime is one time too many. Well, good night then. Elani will know when you are ready and will come to escort you back to your room. We'll begin in the morning."

Slogar had one question that wouldn't wait, so he ventured to ask, "Seelah, who were the other two?" She looked at him for a moment trying to think what *two* he could be asking about. Oh yes, the purification survivors.

"You've met one of them already; Elani of Trilvar. The other, Alesander of Vartuch, left us after five seasons to return to his native planet. He was armed with plans and knowledge for revitalizing his ecosphere, determined to bring his dead planet back to life. He was well disguised and sent a coded confirmation of his arrival. I haven't heard from him since." Slogar was stunned, not by Alesander – he had never heard of him and knew no one from his planet. But Elani. Elani of Trilvar? He had gone to university with two Trilvarians: Vandalen and Elsnor. Vandalen had gone on to become very prominent under Elder Borm's rule, but had met with unfortunate circumstances after the coup. What became of

Elsnor, he had no idea. Could Elani be related to either of these men? Perhaps she was kin to Vandalen; she was tall like he was. Slogar knew Vandalen very well and in truth had much more recent knowledge of him, but for his own safety, he told no one — not even the Elder Woman, though he was fairly sure she knew anyway.

For the next several months, Seelah worked with Slogar to produce remedies for a multitude of illnesses, most of which no one had even thought of in centuries. Some of their medicines were wrought from formulas found in old books; others they designed as new treatments for old illnesses. True to her promise, Seelah also addressed Slogar's weight-related health issues. Each day after meals, Seelah and Slogar took a walkabout through Elani's gardens. They were spectacular. The compound was designed to channel sunlight down into some of the chambers. There was one area that was very reminiscent of the beaches of old. There were coconut and banana trees and plenty of shells, which led Slogar to surmise that sea creatures, including fish, were abundant in the clear blue-green waters that rhythmically lapped the shore. How he would love to have fresh flounder prepared with some of Elani's delicate herbs. The very thought made him hungry.

One day after their mid-day meal, he and Seelah went for their usual stroll, which he found much easier now that he'd lost some weight.

"Seelah," he began, "does Elani ever catch fish for dinner? I'm not complaining, mind you, but we eat mostly tredon and fowl, or vegetables with bread, cheese. Fish would be a nice change, don't you think?"

The Elder Woman wasn't offended, "Yes, it probably would, though I have never asked Elani to prepare any fish. But I will ask her for you."

"Thank you. Uhm, do you think she might like help in catching them?" Slogar's eyes lit up at the thought of fishing again, something he'd not done since he was a child on Ashtar. Gracious as always, Seelah replied, "I'm sure she will be most appreciative for any help you care to give. Just remember that we have bigger fish to fry, pardon the pun." Slogar found that extremely funny and laughed out loud for the first time since he'd been with Seelah. He would never have guessed that the Elder Woman of Silden had a sense of humor, no matter how subtle. The look she gave him let him know she wasn't joking.

Seelah strode ahead, but Slogar sat down on a rocky protrusion by the shore to take in the sunset. That there seemed to be a sunset down here amazed him. How could that be? He could only guess that this was one of the Elder Woman's illusions. Even so, he liked it. There was something infinitely peaceful about this chamber, with its gentle breezes and warm sand. The smell of the salty air invigorated him. He rose to see that Seelah was a tiny speck moving up the beach. He knew that soon it would be time to dine and exercise again. 'Not enough hours in the day,' he thought, 'I still have several papers to review.'

As he caught up to Seelah, she turned and motioned him to a small boat sporting a colorful sail. They walked over to it; Seelah greeted Elani who was on the opposite side, tugging it onto the shore. She no longer wore her long flowing robe, but wore instead what looked to Slogar to be a water-proof uniform. He grabbed the vessel and helped.

"Dr. Slogar would like to go fishing with you, Elani. Do you have the requisite paraphernalia for him?" Elani and Slogar exchanged a glance, instantly knowing that though the Elder Woman was wise, she knew little of fishing.

The tiniest hint of a smile crossed Elani's lips as she replied, "Yes, Ma'am. I believe I do. When would you like to go, Doctor?"

Slogar was quick in his reply, "Tomorrow, if we could. I haven't fished in years. I think it might be relaxing. We have been working very hard. What do you say, Seelah? Do you want to come with us?"

Seelah could think of nothing she would dread more. "I have many more formulas to work out before we can test any new remedies. You two can go in the morning. If you have good fortune, perhaps we'll have some of your catch for lunch." Slogar and Elani finally wrestled the boat in, and the three of them strode to the far end of the beach where the camouflaged door led them back into the main enclave.

The Elder Woman asked Elani to join them that evening for dinner. Slogar had more questions, but struggled with the propriety of asking them. They chatted lightly of tomorrow's fishing adventure. Slogar wondered aloud if the fish were as delicious as the ones he'd eaten as child.

Elani responded, somewhat more coolly than usual, "I do not know what kind of fish you had as a child. These are native to Andalla, so they are probably not the same. However, fish, no matter where they are from, are still fish. They share similar characteristics but distinctive flavors. Some of our fish are so flavorful you may never want Ashtarian fish again."

Slogar knew he needed to correct his blunder before he spoiled his chance to go fishing, so he said, "I'm sure the Andallan fish are every bit as tasty as those of Ashtar, indeed even better. I can't wait to try them." Elani was mollified a little, and graced him with a fleeting smile. Slogar breathed a sigh of relief. He had to be more sensitive. He could see that Elani had worked very hard to nurture all the plants, animals, and yes, fish, here to make sure they were healthy and nutritious. He would be very careful in the future not to compare them with any other. He didn't want her to decide not to take him fishing; but more importantly, he knew had to gain her trust if he was to ever learn of her connection, if one existed, to Elsnor or Vandalen. Seelah could tell that his thoughts had left the present and were going into directions she knew could lead him to some of the answers he had been so desperately seeking.

With a final "Good evening," she left him still seated at the table. Elani rose, "I will be back for you shortly, Doctor." Alone at the table, Slogar gazed at the great portion of roast that lay before him. Though still full of questions and yearning for answers, he lived by the motto of 'waste not, want not.' He reached for yet another serving of the succulent meat. After he had eaten himself into a near coma, Elani re-appeared without a sound.

"As you know, the Elder Woman will not be joining you for your nightly walkabout. Would you like for me to go with you?" Elani asked this as she surveyed the heap of tredon

23

bones on his plate. Slogar didn't want to go, but knew that he'd overeaten and really needed the exercise. Elani sighed. She'd have to clean the dining room later, but she had grown fond of this rather odd doctor and wanted him to regain his health. She smiled shyly and offered him her arm. He chuckled and took it.

So they walked, this time through her hydro garden. About halfway in, the misters engaged, catching them off guard. Elani danced in the mist like a child in the rain. Slogar liked this carefree side of her. He stood watching her delight in the rainbows created by the mist and light, not even caring that he too was getting soaked.

They continued on the walkabout trail that led them back to the main enclave where Elani, once again somber, accompanied him back to his room. There she bade him good night and left him for the evening. Slogar found Elani utterly intriguing. He wanted ask about her father, but instinctively knew the time was not yet right. Perhaps on their fishing expedition tomorrow he would have an opportunity.

The next morning, earlier than he would have liked, he heard the gentle tap on his door and knew that Elani was ready to go. Quickly putting on his robe, he ushered her into his sitting area while he retired to dress for the day. After a few minutes he returned to find Elani sitting perfectly still looking at one of his books. "Ah, you've found my book of ancient surgical techniques. Does this interest you?"

Elani replied, looking up from the book, "Very much. I once was a surgeon." Slogar noticed the long, slender fingers and guessed she must have been good at it. When he also considered her intelligence and calm demeanor, he could see very clearly that she had the makings of a successful surgeon.

Slogar took this as the opening he needed. "Where did you practice, my dear?"

"On Trilvar. I was a pediatric surgeon. So many of our children had deformities residual from the days of excessive drug use among our people; I knew that's where I could make a difference. My father encouraged me in my profession though my mother was worried that I was too tenderhearted." Tenderhearted would not have been a descriptor Slogar would use for her, but then he didn't know her — yet.

He mused aloud, "Trilvar. I went to school with some Trilvarians. What is your father's name?" Elani, who had been speaking easily before, stopped to look at Slogar. She considered how much she should tell him, but decided given their circumstances she would answer him.

"My father is Vandalen. He practiced a different type of medicine. I'm sure you know who he was and what happened to him. But I do not wish to dwell on this right now. Are you ready to catch our lunch?" Slogar had learned all he really needed to know for now and was eager to get back to the beach chamber. Someday he would get the Elder Woman to tell him how she had created this incredibly complex, yet beautiful world. But today, the fish were waiting and Simon Slogar intended to catch them.

Ready for Launch

After ten more months, Slogar left Seelah and Elani. Together they had helped him overcome his craving for ale and had helped him begin to lose some of the excess weight he had carried for so long. He was still a large man, but he was determined to continue to live as Seelah and Elani had taught him. When he took his leave of the Elder Woman, he felt a tug at his heart; she had become something of a mother figure for him, a fact that he found simultaneously comforting and troubling. He promised to return to see her when it was safe. Leaving Elani was harder; what he felt for her was not at all fatherly. He had become genuinely fond of Elani. During their fishing trips, they had gotten to know each other's strengths and flaws. Only Elani's flaws weren't flaws to Slogar; they were endearing quirks that made her infinitely appealing on so many levels. Their brief farewell embrace was the only contact they had ever had, but Slogar and Elani knew that they were forever connected. They had not expected these feelings and knew intellectually that he must leave. With a deep breath of determination, he left these extraordinary women from whom he had learned so much. But there was one thing he had not learned - the thing that had brought him here in the first place. Seelah had not revealed his destiny to him, saying that only God could do that, and only in His time. He knew better than to question Seelah on this point.

Once away from the plains of Silden, he was eager to test some of the remedies he had gotten from Seelah. Slogar traveled into the City of Llanhana where he had heard of a sick child. Once there, he realized that the child had an ancient respiratory ailment called asthma. With the supply of albuterol that he and Seelah had formulated in her secret lab beneath the shanty, he was able to ease the little one's breathing. He stayed with the family a few days, helping the frazzled mother to see that having furry kittels and cubbers around the child was triggering her son's asthma. After a thorough cleaning of the home and purging it of animals, the child recovered. Slogar left a small bottle of albuterol syrup with the mother with the strictest instructions to use the medicine sparingly, not to tell anyone what had happened, and above all, to keep his involvement secret. It was not too long, however, before he was on the run again, as the mother could not contain herself in the telling and retelling of her child's miraculous recovery.

Inevitably, word of this event reached Emperor Jarlod. He was not at all pleased that the truth was being revealed. He was so enamored of himself that he had actually bought into his own hype, at least superficially. Jarlod had made sure that no one questioned his claim of a disease-free empire. That's why he'd gotten rid of the physicians and professors of medicine. But now, he had to deal with this hack. Who was he anyway? Because of this imposter, Jarlod was now forced to face the fact that disease still existed. But he would never admit it. He had to make sure that this information did not go any further. He knew that if it did, the people would probably panic. And that could lead to another coup attempt, this time against him. Thus he reasoned that if the doctor and the family he helped disappeared, then there could be no one from the outside to dispute his word. So, with the exception of the Empire's couriers, all inter-world travel was stopped to and from Andalla until this crisis passed. The family whose little boy had been healed were whisked away and placed in the locked turret of the military base, much to Jarlod's displeasure. He had ordered them eliminated, but his advisors had intervened, convincing him to spare their lives, but not their freedom.

Helgrad

Slogar was in the middle of a very pleasant dream when he was awakened by the sound of his door being blasted open. The Emperor's Troopers crashed into his quarters and dragged him out in the middle of the night, thrust him unceremoniously onto a ship, and transported him to Helgrad — the prison world he had so carefully tried to avoid. He was allowed to take one bag, nothing else. In the lining of this somewhat large bag, he kept hidden his tiny computer that housed his medical research in its drives. He also had hidden among his shaving cream and other necessities, the antidotes and other ancient medicines he and Seelah had formulated.

Helgrad was just one of several very unpleasant events in the Slogar's life. His saving grace was patience. He had enough years and experience on him to know to wait this out. For him, the worst part would be withdrawal. But he'd done it before, and he'd do it now. Who knew? Maybe this time he'd kick his habits for good.

The pod from the ship landed outside his new home. As Slogar exited, he looked at the massive edifice before him. Helgrad stood starkly white against the black mountains it was carved from. He wondered how they'd managed to do that. Its outer walls stood forty feet high and were fifteen feet thick. The tiny windows that let in what little light the prisoners were allowed made the prison look like a giant sieve.

Slogar was herded inside by one of the guards who had captured him. Olsen was shorter than Slogar, but his muscles and wiry frame revealed his incredible strength. He poked Slogar to move him along a bit faster.

Slogar stopped dead still and looked down at the guard, speaking very respectfully, but sternly, "Young man, I am going as fast as I can. Please give me a moment to rest." Olsen, hearing the awful wheezing, looked into the eyes of his charge; he read no threat, so he backed off, but with a warning.

"You will do well to do as you are told here, when you are told to do it. If you do, you may shorten your sentence. If you don't . . . well, let's just say, your issues will be resolved." That said, Olsen, in a rare show of compassion and quite without giving it any thought, decided to help Slogar in the only way he could.

The armed guard at Processing barked, "Who do you have this time, Olsen?"

Olsen replied, "This is Simon Slogar, political prisoner of the Emperor. He is to be kept healthy and to be allowed to have his things, but he is to have no visitors."

Slogar was processed and taken to his cell. On the way, he noticed that the tiny windows on the outside opened beneath the windows into a downward slope to allow the light to illuminate the cells during the day. However, as night rapidly fell, he realized there was no lighting other than dim glow ropes running around the ceiling and floor. He also noticed that most of the cells were quite small, only six feet by eight feet would have been his guess. He was relieved to find that he had been put in a special wing of the prison where he had a larger room, but virtually no interaction with others. 'Thank you, Olsen,' he thought, not knowing yet if that was good or bad. His only conversations would be with the guards, and then only very briefly.

Slogar had never been charged, tried, or convicted. Yet here he sat in this despicable place. He didn't even know how long his sentence was, but figured he'd be blessed to ever have freedom again. So he spent his days studying during the times he knew he was not being observed, eating the food that was pushed into his cell through the feeding slot, and relishing his daily walk. The thought of that made him laugh roundly from time to time, solidifying his guards' notion that he was quite mad.

The weeks turned into months, and the months into nearly a year. By then, he'd gotten used to his routine and looked forward to his one hour in the yard, the only exercise he ever got. Every day the same routine, until one day as he was getting ready to go for his exercise, a different guard strode up to his cell, a handful of papers waving from his fist.

"I don't know how you managed it, Old Man, but I have your release papers. Get your belongings. You're free to go." The words weren't registering fast enough on his brain. He was just about to ask the guard about his morning walkabout, when the fog lifted and he understood. He was free. How and why he didn't know, or care for that matter. He grabbed his books, crammed them into his trunk and followed the guard out of the cell.

Freedom

Once he was sure no one was coming after him to correct a mistaken release, he hurried to the closest village and found a pub. He proceeded to swill as much ale as he could hold without passing out. Everything that Seelah had warned him of concerning his health was forgotten, hopelessly drowned in the bitter ale that at the moment was nectar.

After he had drunk and eaten his fill, he caught the first freighter he could find and headed to Boldoon, a planet known for its easy life and laid back pace. There were beautiful women and plenty of cheap ale. This was Slogar's idea of the perfect place to fly below the radar. If he felt like continuing his research, he could do it in private; if he felt like drinking all day, he could drink all day. As long as he paid his tab, nobody cared. Unfortunately, he didn't know how much longer he would be able to survive on the funds he had with him. Many times he wished he could access his wealth back on Ashtar, but his account had been frozen by the Empire. Frozen was not exactly an accurate description. His inheritance and all other belongings had been confiscated by the Empire when he was sent to Helgrad. By Reglon law, felons were stripped of everything of value the authorities could find as part of their punishment. The Emperor fed his greed under the guise of justice. He had not yet realized that an oppressed, unappreciated people will inevitably become a rebellious people. And that was far more dangerous than any other threat to the Empire.

Slogar had thought when he left Helgrad under the cover of darkness for this planet, the worst was behind him. Quickly, he discovered that his life here on Boldoon was the worst yet. He was thought of as a useless, old man who did nothing except eat, drink, and sleep. He had come to Boldoon seeking a place where he might just exist, maybe even begin to regain some sense of the old Slogar. Instead, he had found that this world was indeed without need of his knowledge and experience. In the beginning he had tried to fit into one of the preferred Boldoonian professions but was unable to master law, mineral technology, or politics. So he began to eat and drink; both activities he had long since mastered. Each day he drank himself into a peaceful oblivion, starting when he woke just as the day was breaking and not stopping until he collapsed in his own sweaty, drunken stench at the Boor's Nad Inn. This was the last of many sleazy establishments Slogar chose to patronize, mainly because all the others had stopped his credit and not so politely ejected his stinking hulk from their premises.

It was in this comfortable sty that Commander Michael Camdus found him slumped over his platter of tredon bones. Though Camdus had communicated with him recently, it had been many years since he had actually seen Dr. Simon Slogar. Except for his increased bulk, Slogar hadn't changed.

"Slogar. Wake up, you old buzzard. You were supposed to meet me at the dock at 9:00 this morning. I thought maybe you had been held up getting supplies. But when my ensign checked with the supply houses, he learned no one had seen you. For that matter, no one had ever heard of you! I knew that you'd chicken out. You're a spineless old fart." Slogar still didn't respond, so Camdus nudged him, "Hey, are you listening to me or what?"

"What." Slogar burped the word with a snort.

Camdus could feel his anger rising, but knew that it was important to get through to Slogar without antagonizing him any further. Slogar's self-pity was disgusting, but he was the only medical doctor on any of the Reglon Empire's worlds or its asteroid colonies, which were like mini-worlds, except that they depended on the true worlds for almost all of their necessities.

For his part, Slogar did not appreciate Cam calling him up, prodding old memories, memories Slogar had tried to drown, though they proved to be very good swimmers. Even through his ale-fogged brain, he thought yet again about his erstwhile journey to where he was now. It was only by pure stubbornness that Slogar had become a doctor, with Seelah's help, of course.

"Look, Commanner," Slogar groused, "I nefer wanted to be a dockor. I'uz gonna be a perfessor at one a 'em biggg univershities, not shome podung school where I woodn make 'nough to live on. Ya know, back then, it was all about money and tresp..preswege… Ah hell, you know whad I mean."

Cam offered his guess, "It was about money and prestige?"

"Yeah, thash whad I said. Bu' I din nee' th' money; it wuz th' power I want'd. More money, more power, plain and shimple. Bud shomewhere along the way I musta los' my mind 'cause I wuz more attracted to he'ping everyone, not jush th' priverleged few. I was one of 'em priverleged few, ya know. So why'd I care about th' lesh forshunut? And look where tha' go' me?" His words were really slurring now, "I can't efen ge' drung anymore wifout being harashed by one o' the Empersh's flungies."

Camdus was sick of Slogar's bellyaching; and when Slogar was drinking, it seemed like that's all he wanted to do. "Don't blame me for your choices. You're the one who wanted to become a doctor, licensed or not, so just look in the mirror next time you want to complain. On one point, you're almost right: I am one of the Emperor's soldiers, but I'm nobody's flunky - or 'flungy' as you put it. Let's just get this crap out here and now so we can move on. Tell me the rest of your story. I'm listening. But how about taking this transcap so I can understand you?"

Slogar, though offended, took the pill. In a few seconds, he had sobered up enough to share this part of his life with someone. If Camdus was willing to listen, then Slogar was willing to talk.

After a while, Cam became aware that he had not been listening, so he tuned back in to hear Slogar wrapping up his story. " ....of medicine without financial worry. So that's how I became about as knowledgeable as any professor of medicine could without benefit of formal education and practical experience. Yet out of desperation and an inexplicable sense of knowing I had to master medicine, I started on my journey to become a doctor in every regard."

Camdus interrupted, "But surely you knew there would be no certifications? No way to have a medical practice, right?" Slogar nodded affirmatively.

"So why do it?" Cam asked.

Slogar had asked himself that a thousand times. "I decided that there must be some part of the vast Reglon Empire that was not as advanced as the political leaders would have everyone believe. My research pointed me to the tiny world of Andalla or so I thought until I realized that Seelah had willed me there, but that's another story. I practiced ancient medicine briefly until Helgrad and now the same Emperor who threw me in prison wants my help. Well," Simon said with particular venom, "Jarlod can just go …'

Just as Slogar was ready to verbally skewer the Emperor, Camdus interrupted him. Cam was fed up and was not inclined to hear anymore.

"Okay, okay. We don't have time for your unabridged autobiography or your opinion of the Emperor. As you know from the Emperor's communication with you — don't roll your eyes at me —Creedor is in serious trouble. This epidemic has baffled even the wisest of Jarlod's advisors. None of them has ever seen an epidemic. For that matter, none of them has ever seen even a simple 20th century disease like museles."

"That's 'measles,'" Slogar corrected.

"Museles, measles, whatever. The bottom line is that you're the only person we know of in the Empire who has any experience with disease of any kind, and now we have this epidemic destroying what's left of the population of Creedor." Camdus paused before continuing. "We have all this data from our ancient history archives and it's meaningless to everyone. Everyone except you, that is. Now, will you come on your own or do I have to drag your sorry behind out of this dump and have you escorted to the ship?"

Slogar was getting tired of people putting saving the Empire on his shoulders. If this was his destiny, he wanted no part of it. Who exactly did they think he was, anyway? And how exactly did they expect him to be of any help? One transcap wasn't enough to get him through the headache he felt coming on. He brushed aside the greasy ale mug and reached for another pill, swallowing it without benefit of water. Camdus began counting. At fifteen, Slogar looked up with piercing, brown eyes that were no longer glazed over with the onset of stabbing pain. When he spoke there was a leaden quality to his voice. "The Creedorians are better off without a doctor at all than one who doesn't seem to know what he's doing anymore. Most of what I haven't drowned in ale is just theory and that won't do them any good. The last thing they need is a broken-down, besotted has-been telling them what to do to get well. I'm not even sure that I will recognize the ailment once I get there — if I get there. I just think that you're banking on a loser. If I do go along with it, the Creedorians will be the real losers; they'll be risking their lives when maybe the disease will run its course and the Creedorians will recover without interference. Why don't you just go on without me? My life here is just fine anyway, just the way it is." He wiped his greasy hands on his ale-soaked outershirt.

"Spare me, Slogar. Sure, your life looks really great. I mean just look around you. You haven't had a decent meal in months. Your social life is non-existent. The most beautiful women in the Empire are all around you and you stay too drunk to notice. Not that any of them would have anything to do with you. Come on, Slo, look at you. You haven't had a bath in so long that they aren't making the same kind of soap anymore. And your clothes are so filthy that they could probably stand alone, if you'd ever take them off. Not to mention your belly. When's the last time you saw your feet? Do you even remember what kind of shoes you're wearing?"

"Hey, all right. Enough. And I do know what kind of shoes I'm wearing, wise guy."

Camdus couldn't resist. "What kind?"

Until this very moment Slogar had no clue how obese he had become. "Damn it, Cam. I *don't* know; I can't even see them. See, you've made my point for me. How do you expect a man who can't even see his own shoes to save a planet?"

Cam hadn't expected this turn in the argument, but he was not to be so easily dissuaded. "All right, you know, truth is truth, but I didn't mean to be quite so blunt. But if you come with me, I think we can help you get in better shape in no time, especially once we get moving. And we have got to get moving; no more arguments. Deal?" But Slogar had begun to tremble violently, not from emotion but from withdrawal. Cam offered Slogar another transcap to calm him. Slogar took it without even acknowledging that he had seen it. He had trouble admitting that he was hooked – again.

But hooked he was and at this moment Camdus was tempted to take Slogar up on his invitation to leave him alone. But instead he said, "Come off it, Slo. You know, you used to have a promising future. All that knowledge can't have been washed away, no matter how much ale you've swilled. As to the epidemic going away on its own, give me a break. Since last month, more than 2,000 Credooorians have died a tortuous death. We've got a cruiser to catch at eleven tonight. That doesn't give us much time. So how about it, Slo; you coming with us, or do I have to let the Emperor know that you decline his invitation to join us on this mission?"

Slogar wanted to tell Camdus and the rest of these "you can save the Empire" fanatics where to go and how to get there. But that wasn't an option. "All right, all right. I'll be there. Now don't you have somewhere to be?" Camdus knew that dealing with an alcoholic was a gamble, but it was the only one he had. Just as the door to the inn closed, Camdus heard Slogar shout, "Barkeep, another here."

Unknown Danger

Slogar wasn't by himself in looking like a tredon bull that had seen far too many seasons. Though her engines, electronics, and weaponry had been updated, the cruiser looked like it too had seen better days. Its once flawless glaze was now scratched and pocked, its call letters barely visible. Some pilot in years past had painted the picture of a gorgeous two-headed wench on the side. Obviously a Talean beauty. 'Oh well, to each his own . . . .' Camdus was brought out of his mental ramblings by a gruff grunt and a shove from one of the Boldoonian laborers straining under the loaded crate of supplies.

"Watch where you're going, you son of a she-dog!" Camdus swore at the sweating laborer. "Are you blind, or just dumb? And be careful with that crate. Those supplies had better be intact or you won't be. You got that?" The worker carefully placed the crate to the side, turned to face Camdus, and spoke in a controlled voice.

"The name is Grunden, Commander Camdus. I will carry your crates as ordered, but I will not be talked to as if I were one of your sluggard dogs, much less the son of a she-dog. Is *that* understood ... Sir?"

Camdus considered this man — Grunden — for the first time. How had he overlooked this one when had sought men of mettle for the voyage to Creedor? Obviously here was a man with integrity. And his sheer strength was evident even beneath the bulky laborer's overshirt. 'I wonder why a man such as this has been relegated to the position of common laborer. Most of them are too ignorant to be insulted. Or get in out of the rain, for that matter.' Studying him, Camdus tried to place Grunden in his mind. His face and name were familiar, but he just could not remember. 'Well, it'll come to me sooner or later, I suppose.' He then addressed Grunden in a more respectful tone.

"Tell me, Grunden, why aren't you among our fighters or builders? What brought you here, of all places?" Grunden looked away. The western sol was riding low just before dusk, giving the sky an aura of blue and purple, tinged with feathers of green. The beauty of dusk never disappointed Grunden as he sought peace in it.

He spoke quietly, yet there was an undertone to his voice that put Camdus on his guard. "Commander, not all grunts are mindless fools. Some of us chose to come into this service. And those of us who did have reasons for keeping a low profile."

"What reasons? Who are you loyal to, Grunden?" Cam had his hand on his side arm, ready to use it if necessary. Grunden studied Camdus. He had already said too much; he hoped that his spies had been correct in their assessment of the commander.

"We — I am loyal to the Empire. Yet since Jarlod came into power, I have had to struggle to remain that way. I keep reminding myself that he's just one ...."

Camdus interrupted, "One what? He's our Emperor; loyalty to him is mandatory." A group of recruits came into view tramping up the boarding ramp. Both Camdus and Grunden became silent, waiting for them to pass before continuing.

"Look, Commander," Grunden said in a low voice, "take me with you and I'll tell you everything you want to know, only not out here; it isn't safe."

Camdus adhered to the 'keep-your-friends-close-and-your-enemies-closer' school of thought, so he said, "All right, Grunden. I'm conscripting you into the Emperor's Fleet Service, effective immediately. We'll talk after we're underway. Until then, stay close. Understood?"

"Understood, Sir."

How Camdus hated to return to the stench of Creedor; its mass graves were filling by the hour. Death was everywhere; it seemed to permeate one's body, leaving nothing but a hollow cavern of fear and despair. But Emperor Jarlod had personally given Camdus the order. Now it looked as if he would have to go without the physician. Slogar had not shown up, and they could not afford to wait for him. There was other business they had to take care of in Clandil, anyway. 'Enough,' he thought. 'I should have known he wouldn't come. He's too far gone. Well, maybe it's for the best.' He picked up his trooper's helmet, dusting it with his sleeve. The ship was almost loaded; all he needed now was to contact the pilot to make sure the preflight check had been successfully completed. Who knew what they would find this time; but whatever was behind the Creedorian epidemic had to be dangerous. With these thoughts in mind, he headed for the bridge. On his way, he stopped to make sure the boarding port was locked. It was then that he heard the most awful wheezing imaginable. Peering out into the growing darkness, he saw Slogar lumbering up the ramp which had just started moving away from the ship. Camdus hit the ramp interrupt switch to stop its movement and return it to the ship, nearly knocking the doctor off his feet in the process. He noted that Slogar was carrying a small black case and tugging at a rope slung over one massive shoulder. A very large trunk on wheels was tethered to the rope.

"You wouldn't leave without me, now would you, Commander? It takes a little more time to get a rusty old relic like me moving. You know, you really should be more patient and have a little consideration for the infirmities of your elders," he huffed at Camdus, who stepped onto the ramp and was nearly knocked off his feet as the old man struggled with his paraphernalia.

"Slogar, sometimes you are such an ass. You could have let me know you were on the way. Too bad you're under the Emperor's protection." Camdus mused, 'Amazing how fast a man's worth can change in this Empire.' Still, Camdus felt the urge to belt Slogar, but thought better of it. After all, Slogar was a physician — the physician — and the Emperor had ordered Camdus to get him on that cruiser one way or another. This way he would not have to try to explain to Emperor Jarlod why he had disobeyed a direct order. After his meeting with Slogar, he thought that he was more trouble than he was worth. And up until this very moment, Camdus had been prepared to leave Slogar behind if he didn't show up and then to report that he had failed, taking whatever punishment Jarlod chose to prescribe. He fully intended, however, to use whatever means necessary to drag Slogar right along with him into whatever slime pit he was assigned. Slogar wouldn't know where he was, he was so used to dismal ale holes. And when he sobered up enough to know that there wouldn't be any more ale .... 'Oh well,' Camdus thought, 'I don't have to worry about that now.'

Camdus finally was able to align the large trunk properly to get it through the door. He swore silently, sweat pouring down his back. He stood up again, pulled the doctor's belongings inside, and barked, "Haul your worthless ass in here now, Slogar. I've had just about all of you I can take for one day."

Just then, Grunden came back to where Camdus was to see what was holding up the flight. Grunden saw the filthy hulk of a man who was obviously giving the commander grief. He stepped between Commander Camdus and the intruder, glowering at the stranger.

Grunden spoke directly to the Commander, "Sir, do you want me to take care of this riffraff for you?"

"This riffraff, as you so aptly put it, is Dr. Simon Slogar of Ashtar, more recently of the Boor's Nad Inn on Boldoon. Despite his unseemly appearance, Dr. Slogar is here at the request of the Emperor himself; he has been assigned the task of ending the epidemic on Creedor." Camdus paused a moment as he watched Grunden's expression go from one of hostility to one of total amazement. Grunden, for his part, knew now where he had seen this one before, but a physician? How could that be possible?

"Grunden, please help the doctor to his quarters next to mine. I'm in OQ2. The doctor will be in OQ3. Dr. Slogar, I will assign an assistant to work directly with you and provide you with whatever you need for your scientific or medical pursuits. If there is anything else that you may require, Doctor, you must see me directly. Do you understand?" This last statement was delivered as Cam sent a penetrating stare that seemed to bore into Slogar's very brain.

Slogar responded, somewhat pettishly, "I understand all too well what you mean. No ale. That won't be a problem. I can assure you. Now, if you'll show me to my quarters."

He turned as if to walk down the corridor, but Cam clutched his elbow. He'd noticed several bulges in Slogar's filthy cloak. He reached in and removed the hidden ale bottles, which he handed to Grunden. "Mr. Grunden, please dispose of these. Dr. Slogar won't be needing them."

"You can't take my belongings. Who do you think you are? Give me those!" Slogar made a lunge for the bottles that Grunden held tightly in his hands. The old doctor tripped over his large case landing with a loud thud on his well-padded backside. He knew defeat when it stared him in the face. "I hope you have enough transcaps on board, Commander," Slogar said, as he took Cam's arm and with great effort, pulled himself up.

Camdus waited for him to get an even footing, then he reminded Slogar, "I am the Commander of this ship, and I decide who brings what on board. And you, Sir, will not be bringing any unauthorized spirits on this ship. Do you understand?"

By this time Slogar had regained his composure and responded, "I understand perfectly, Commander. And as to the assistant, I will welcome one, if that's what you really mean. But I don't much like the idea of a body guard."

"We'll see," clipped Cam. "Grunden, when you've finished, please report to my quarters."

"Yes, Sir," Grunden replied. He'd be relieved to get this interview over with.

Mission within a Mission - Grunden's Story

The purple iris sky had already begun to darken when the ship launched on its journey to Creedor. Normally the beginning of a new mission spawned excitement among the crew; this time it was different. The shadow of Creedor's unknown dangers loomed in each mind as they hurtled through space. Even the stars seemed to pull away as they went, shimmering cowards of the night. After Grunden had gotten the doctor settled in, he stowed his own gear and the doctor's confiscated ale. Grunden was pleased that his quarters were quite spacious, which was almost unheard of for a noncom. His room, OQ4, adjoined Slogar's. Grunden appreciated this strategy. After all, it made sense to keep the doctor surrounded by men proven in battle. But the Commander didn't know that, at least not as far as Grunden knew. It was almost time for his meeting with Camdus. He hoped he'd find out more then.

The door swooshed shut behind Grunden. He noted that the Commander's quarters were spartan, but about the same size as his and Slogar's. Camdus motioned him to sit in one of the simple leather chairs near him. On a table in front of him were small plates of fruit, vegetables, and something that looked like dried meat. Two tall mugs of a golden liquid were on either side of the table. Camdus looked at Grunden, and indicated the food with a nod toward the table. "Let's eat while we talk. I'm sure you're as hungry as I am after the work we've put in today." Grunden settled in with a plate of food, which was surprisingly good. Either that or it had been such a long time since he'd had anything other than canned rations, that pretty much anything else would taste good. He sipped the beverage, ale, not his favorite but tolerable. But as the ale slid down his throat, he felt an easy warmth spreading over him. Until that moment he hadn't realized just how to-the-bone cold he'd gotten working outside on this frigid, overcast day. Leaning back in his chair, he began to relax. For some time neither man spoke. Then Camdus rose, pushed a button and sweet strains of classical music filled the room. He had developed this habit years ago when he worked covertly on Ashtar for the new Emperor.

"Now then, Grunden. Why did you risk your position by talking to me? You are aware that there are more than a few commanders who would have you thrown into the brig for such insolence."

Grunden took a deep breath and said, "Yes, Sir. I'm well aware of that. But things have changed of late. All of us who can, need to find ways to get to Creedor. As to why I chose you, I did so only after closely considering everything I know about you. We did our research, Commander. I decided I had to trust the intel, even though you might have been one of them." Grunden saw that Camdus was still very much confused. "You see, our mission is more urgent now. I had no choice but to risk you throwing me in the brig for insubordination, but I had to get your attention. By the way, thank you for *not* throwing me in the brig. I've been there before; never for long, but I don't much want to go again. Look, Commander, I can't afford to get locked up, even for a little while - not now anyway."

Camdus was struggling to make sense of what Grunden was saying. Who exactly was 'them'? "Listen, if you're trying to tell me something, just spit it out. There's a world on the path to total extinction if we don't get there and do something to stop the plague that is ravaging its inhabitants.

Now, what I don't understand is while every sane person on Creedor is trying to get around the quarantine to escape, you and your group are trying to get around the same quarantine to get to Creedor. I don't have time to play guessing games. So you're just going to have to cut out the bull and tell me what you're up to - now."

Grunden realized that Camdus was focused on the epidemic. 'Could it be that he was unaware of the intruders?'

"Commander, the epidemic is only one of your challenges on Creedor. I don't know everything; however, I can say that our intelligence reports indicate that there are outsiders deep within the planet, most likely stealing trizactl. Who and why, we don't know — yet. We have reason to believe that the disease that's killing the planet life was deliberately released by these invaders. That's the best answer I can give you right now. I trusted you, Commander. Now I'm asking that you trust me."

Cam sat motionless, trying to digest this new information. Intruders stealing trizactl could well interfere with their fight to save the Creedorians from the plague. And what if this disease were genetically engineered to have no antidote? He could not entertain these thoughts for they indicated certain defeat. His gut told him Grunden was trustworthy; he prayed that was the case.

"Will you accept the position of assistant to Dr. Slogar? His safety is of utmost importance to the fate of Creedor, perhaps ours as well. At least as far as the plague is concerned." Grunden considered the request without answering, as Cam sank back into his chair and let the ale take hold, easing him into thoughts so deep Grunden sensed it best not to disturb him. He knew better than to express disagreement, even if he felt it.

After a bit, he gave Camdus the reply he knew was required, "I appreciate the assignment, Commander. Something about the old doctor intrigues me." 'Besides,' he thought, 'Who knows what kinds of things I can learn from this pseudo-relic.' He knew one thing for sure and that was that Dr. Slogar was nobody's fool, even though it was obvious he often chose to play a fool's role.

"You know, Commander, I've seen Dr. Slogar on several occasions at the Boor's Nad Inn. Every now and then, the regulars set him up with rounds of ale so they could watch his drunken antics. But one evening, I saw him huddled with a heavily robed figure. I tried to eavesdrop, but I could only hear bits and pieces of the conversation, not enough to know exactly what the two were talking about. But I gathered that they were talking about the Emperor and his henchmen. The robed figure was so totally masked that the only thing I could see was the thin pale right hand which bore a fiery diamond mounted in gold and worn on the index finger. Its expert craftsmanship was undeniable. The twin serpents entwined to hold the diamond had perfectly matched rubies for eyes. Beneath each eye, the letter "V" shown in silver inlays."

Camdus listened more intently for he knew that Grunden was describing the ring worn by Vandalen of Trilvar, once Reglon's Supreme Wizard, now exiled on Dartal, the dark, forbidding underworld that orbited the even darker planet of Killund.

"You're sure of this?" Camdus asked.

Grunden gave Camdus a look that registered the insult he felt. He let the Commander know that he was so sure he had sent scouts out at once to discover the identity of the robed figure, to no avail. Grunden was well versed in Reglon history and knew for a fact that a ring exactly like this had been worn by the Trilvarian wizard Vandalen. But reports from all agents indicated that Vandalen was indeed still on Dartal. This had to be one of his lieutenants. But what was he doing on Boldoon? And what could he possibly want with the village drunk? Now Grunden was beginning to see through the haze, though not too clearly. At least now he knew that Slogar was not a mere drunk. He was a physician; and according to Commander Camdus, the only hope for the Creedorians in their desperate battle with this unknown disease. But that did not explain the Trilvarian lieutenant, unless ....

Camdus and Grunden sat in the dim light, both deep in thought. The music no longer registered in either man's consciousness. In their semi-relaxed state, they struggled with what they knew and even more, what they needed to know for survival as they sped ever closer to Creedor and whatever challenges it would surely bring.

"If there's nothing else, Sir, I'll go check on Dr. Slogar."

"Thank you, Mr. Grunden. That is all for this evening. We'll continue this conversation again tomorrow same time." Cam couldn't shake the feeling that he'd seen Grunden somewhere before. He was sure it would come to him. He just hoped that when he remembered he would not regret taking him on this mission.

Grunden's Story Continues

After a very tiring day, Grunden reported to the Commander's quarters to continue his interview. With permission to enter granted to Grunden, the Commander's door slid open. Camdus motioned Grunden again to the same chair, with an even better meal laid out before him. He thought, 'Maybe I should become like Scheherazade, the ancient storyteller. The Commander spreads a decent table. I wouldn't mind eating here every day.' Grunden looked up from the meal spread before him to see Commander Camdus watching him intently. He did not flinch under the Commander's steady gaze, yet he was not comfortable either. He sighed, thinking 'May as well get this over with.'

"Now Grunden, I'm still trying to make heads or tails out of what you told me last night about Slogar's behavior on Boldoon. But for now, tell me what you're trying to accomplish and who you're working with?"

Grunden hardly knew where to start, but he knew he'd better try. "Commander, Creedor is not the only planet with unregistered visitors. About six months ago, I was serving on the Emperor's Orbital Patrol on Reglon Major. My unit was charged with ensuring that the Elsnith Oasis was used only by the Royals and their guests, no one else. Late one evening after an especially boring watch, I started to pack it in and report back to my quarters. Just as I was about to enter my pod, I heard something beyond the trees to the west. I froze, straining to hear it again. Officer Salzer, who was on watch with me, didn't hear anything and wanted to go. I told him we needed to go see if we could find what made that noise. He didn't want to, but we were under orders to investigate anything suspicious. So we went on foot about a half mile, careful to stay in the darkest shadows. We saw maybe a dozen hooded figures, their dormant invisi-shields lying on the ground. Just behind them was a sheer cliff that seemed to be solid rock. Yet the intruders disappeared one by one through an opening that closed up after the last one and his shield were inside. We went cautiously up to the cliff for a closer look. There was no sign of an entryway. How they got in, we had no idea."

Cam interrupted Grunden's story by asking, "What did Command say when you reported it?"

"We talked about making the report and even began initial contact with Command."

Cam was getting irritated again. "Did you make the report? A simple *yes* or *no* will do."

Grunden answered, "No, Sir."

"All right. Now explain, Mr. Grunden." Camdus was a stickler for procedure. This had better be good.

Grunden began again, "You'd think with all we've gone through and all the other worlds Jarlod has ticked off, he'd be more receptive to any report of unauthorized activity, no matter how bizarre. But it seems that our Emperor is more interested in preventing peasants from visiting Elsnith than in protecting the Empire. At any rate, we both knew of others who'd made similar reports and were subsequently removed from duty. So, we didn't. Right or wrong – we didn't."

Cam took a long drink of his ale, and then he asked, "So let me get this straight. You and your patrol partner decided to save your own hide rather than follow procedure? That seems inconsistent with the kind of soldier I took you to be."

"Commander, think about it — if we 'disappeared' like some of our comrades, who would be left to fight, if a fight was needed."

"I understand your reasons, Mr. Grunden, but what I want to know is how what you're doing now ties in to this mission to Creedor? It does, doesn't it?"

"Yes, Commander, it definitely does. From that night on I knew that something was really out of place. More than that, I guess you could say I had a gut feeling that we're in danger. How much and what kind of danger, I didn't know; I still don't for that matter. But to get back to how this ties in: I quietly pulled together a handpicked group of men, who like me, love all our worlds and want them to be safe so that we can live in peace. Most of the men are soldiers who were relieved of duty after reporting suspicious activity. It wasn't too hard to convince them to join me."

Camdus sat quietly for a moment before he spoke. "So you've formed a rebel band to fight clandestinely to save Reglon Empire. Would that be a safe guess?"

"Yes, Sir, that is as good as any. There aren't many of us, but we're not afraid to fight; and we are fiercely loyal to the people, not Jarlod. If Reglon Major and now Creedor are under attack, Boldoon will probably be next. We don't know how much time we have. We don't know exactly what we're facing. But we know that whoever they are, they have extraordinary powers. If they meant no harm, they'd have registered and would not come and go under cover of darkness and invisi-shield. We need your help, Commander. You have contacts among very gifted and loyal people. It will take all the talent, courage, and skill we can muster. Please think about it, Commander. I know your mission is important, but somehow, I think this is just as important."

Camdus considered what Grunden had told him; then he said, "You have proof of this?" Grunden affirmed this by passing a tiny computer card to him. "Everything we have is on this disk."

Camdus held the tiny revelation in his hand, then said, "There's just one more thing I want to know: Who did these officers make the reports to?"

Without hesitation, Grunden said, "They all reported to Elder Tomer Arking."

"Elder Arking? Mr. Grunden, are you sure it wasn't Elder Spetch?"

"Yes, Sir, I'm sure it was Elder Arking." Camdus would put nothing past Spetch, but Tomer Arking?

Camdus had always thought very highly of him; he had been a close friend of Cam's father. Now he needed to find out more about him. He told Grunden that he would look into it; then he dismissed him for the evening.

'Elder Arking. Hmm. He's always been an advocate for the citizens. What is he hiding?' Cam touched his computer, which sprang instantly to life. He popped the disk into the port and sat back to see what was on it, but not before he poured himself another drink. He listened to his whirring computer as it read the disk. Soon he'd know what Grunden was talking about, hopefully. And after he had, he'd find out what the Empire buzz said about Elder Arking. Finally, when he had as much information as he could glean, he'd call his dad to learn as much as he could about Tomer Arking, the man.

As he sat back down with his glass in hand, Camdus continued to ponder the unsettling conversation he'd just had with Grunden. He found himself in the position of either trusting or eliminating Grunden. Elimination was at least for the present out of the question since Camdus still didn't know enough about his group: Were they really who Grunden said? How many were there? Why did they really organize? What did they think they could do? And to whom? Maybe the disk would provide some of the answers. If not, he'd just have to keep a wary eye on Grunden; unless Slogar could unlock the secret of the disease and find its cure, their chances of getting off Creedor alive were pretty slim anyway.

The disk was a collection of secret documents and video clips of suspicious activity on several planets, but mostly on Creedor, and one from an abandoned airship landing site on Boldoon. Camdus could see now why Grunden had begun his own counter-offensive. The people on the clips were armed with some pretty powerful weapons, some of which he'd never seen before. Further, they seemed to appear and disappear at will, something that, as far as he knew, even the most powerful wizards of Reglon had yet to master. He secured his computer, and locked the disk in his safe. He could not dismiss what he'd just learned. Cam knew the disease on Creedor had to be stopped, but now he had to fight . . . who? He'd recognized the Q'Aron uniforms, but there were other video clips with intruders of unknown origin.

His head felt like it was about to explode, the throbbing was so intense. Cam hadn't endured one of these headaches in years. Lying down on his bed, he closed his eyes and tried to rest, but he could not turn off his thoughts. He gave up. There was a stack of old journals with news clippings and photos strewn on his table. Cam picked one of them up and began re-reading the articles, studying each picture. He turned a page and felt a jolt of recognition. There staring up at him was the face of Grunden, Admiral Maximus Grunden to be exact. At his knee was a young boy, listed as Jacar, the Admiral's son. Cam was amazed at how much he looked like his father, even as a youngster. After Elder Borm was overthrown, the Admiral and all the other Counselors had dropped out of the public eye. Everyone assumed that they had been encouraged to retire and chose to live out their days as quietly as possible. What if that was not the case? Cam picked up his communicator, got a secure channel, and called his father.

Camdus Seeks Information

Willem's voice bore that deep baritone that demanded respect. Though for Cam, respecting his father was more out of love than obligation. His father, Willem Camdus, had been a humble shop keeper to everyone but Cam. When Cam was growing up, he thought no one was smarter or stronger than his dad. Sometimes Cam had pretended to be a soldier; the elder Camdus couldn't help laughing at his little boy's antics. It was only after Cam entered the Academy that he began to hear stories of his dad's bravery when he served in the military under Elder Borm's rule. He and Tomer had both served for a time under Admiral Grunden. Cam hoped his father's experience with the Admiral would prove helpful.

As to Cam's entering the military, his father wasn't surprised when Michael applied to the Academy. His mother was another story; she was not happy about it at all. She could not bear the thought of her son going into harm's way. She had not liked the separations that stretched throughout her husband's years in the military and absolutely did not want her son walking in those shoes. Inevitably, though, Michael was accepted, and after a time shipped out.

Mrs. Camdus had cried herself sleep after he left, but she kept up a brave face until he was well out of sight. "I just wish you had taken the time to counsel him, Will," she pouted.

"Don't worry, Rose. The package I gave him before he left will help him more than any lecture I could have given him. I told him not to use it until he had run out of ideas."

Rose nearly shouted, "What kind of help is that? He may be dead before he knows he needs it." Willem didn't dare point out that she was being illogical. He knew better.

The communicator alerted Willem of a call. He touched the answer button; Cam's face popped up on the screen. "Hi, Dad. You got a minute?" Willem detected an urgent undertone in his son's voice.

"I do. What's on your mind, Son?"

Cam had struggled with how to ask what he needed to know without putting his father at risk. "Dad, I need to ask you some questions about a couple of your old friends, Tomer Arking and Admiral Maximus Grunden. You knew them both pretty well when you were in the military, didn't you?"

Willem thought this a strange question, but answered as best he could. "Yes, I knew them. The Admiral was the kind of leader that men don't mind following. He ordered his troops into battle, but he was right there among them. He never asked a soldier to do anything he couldn't or wouldn't do himself. I'd follow him again, if he needed me." That was comforting for Cam to hear; his instinct about the younger Grunden was most likely right. "Now Tomer, he's a different story. He's as good as gold, but though an adequate soldier, he seemed more scholarly, if you know what I mean. He could recite the details of any battle from any war, but fighting was not his strong suit. It was this grasp of strategic warfare and logistics that made him an effective officer. His forte was giving effective orders to the soldiers under his command. For him, having physical military skill was not as important as using his extensive knowledge of military procedure and warfare. I'm pretty sure that's what helped him to rise to the rank of admiral." Willem was unsure what Tomer Arking had to do with his son, but he intended to find out. "Is he all right? I haven't seen him since Borm was overthrown. Now it's your turn, Michael. What's going on?"

"Well, Dad. It seems that Elder Arking is connected to the disappearance of some soldiers and for some others being mustered out of the service. Why do you think he'd do that?"

Willem considered the information his son had provided in his questions and decided he didn't have enough to answer. "Son, I guess it'd depend on what the soldiers did — what did they do or fail to do that would have prompted Tomer to take such drastic action? But first, let me tell you. I've known Tomer Arking for most of my life, and just as sure as I am he would relieve a malinger of duty, he would NOT make a soldier disappear. He's an honorable man, Michael."

Cam was afraid that he'd offended his father, who was known for his fierce loyalty to friends as well as family. "Dad, I'm not accusing Elder Arking of any misdeeds. I'm just trying to get to the bottom of why the scouts who've reported unauthorized activity to him have either lost their posts or have never been heard of again."

Willem paused; then he went on. "Are you sure these reports were made directly to Tomer? You know he has an assistant who screens all communications to him." In fact, Cam had not known that and doubted that Grunden knew it either. It made perfect sense, when he thought of it. What high ranking official in the Empire didn't have an assistant?

Cam answered his father, "That's something I don't know, but I'll try to find out. Do you still have friends on Reglon Major, especially among the Emperor's Council?" Willem found this conversation troubling, but knew he had to try to help his son.

"Well, as you know, Tomer and I grew up together, so maybe a call on him during a visit to Capitol City in the next few weeks wouldn't raise any suspicions. Once I've talked to him, maybe I'll be able to answer your questions."

"Dad, we may not have a few weeks to get to the bottom of this problem. I really need for you to try to get this information for me now. But I want you to be careful. There is much more subterfuge going on in the Empire than soldiers being relieved of duty or sent away." Willem appreciated the gravity of his son's warning.

"Now, Michael, thanks for the head's up, but please remember that your old man was a pretty accomplished soldier in his day."

"I know, Dad. I just don't want you to take this task too lightly. Just make sure that you only speak to Tomer, and don't let him know why you're visiting him; at least until you're satisfied that he has no part of what's going on, anyway. Please be careful, and get back to me via this secure channel. Tell Mom I love her and will see you all as soon as I can. Thanks, Dad."

"Don't thank me just yet, Son. Let's wait and see what I find out first." Camdus wished his father good luck and signed off.

Cam gets a Warning

Cam was awakened by a beeping at his side. He looked over and saw a message was waiting for him on his communicator. Cam didn't recall nodding off, but knew that he must have done just that. He'd have to do something about that, but right now he didn't have time to sleep. The message was a mass communication from Emperor's Deputy Director of Intergalactic Warfare. Cam noted that it was encrypted. Cam hated encryption, though he knew that there must be a very good reason for using it, especially over secure lines. The message was a warning: Be vigilant, intruders have been reported. 'Humph,' Cam groused, 'Tell me something I don't know.' What he really needed to know was more practical, like how many, what weapons; were there other Empire Cruisers in the area to help? Typical bungling by this preening Emperor seemed to be the rule of the day. Cam could think these things, but would never, under any circumstances, say them. He might not like some of Jarlod's decisions, but he was still their leader and they had to respect that office, if not the man.

Cam thought it time to visit his erstwhile charge, Dr. Simon Slogar. He'd not spent any time with him at all since launch, so now was as good a time as any to find out what the old man knew. He touched the door panel that alerted the occupant that a visitor was waiting for permission to enter. Slogar was still having trouble with all the modern technology, but did remember that to say, "Enter." The door didn't open. He said it again, still nothing. Exasperated, he got up and touched the open button. After the door tightly closed behind Camdus, he greeted the doctor with a serious look.

"All right now, Cam. Don't look at me that way. I just haven't had time to tidy up. Oh, and thanks for the nice quarters. They're a sight better than the corner table at the Boor's Nad Inn."

"You're welcome; but that's not what concerns me. What have you been doing since we left Boldoon? I haven't heard a peep from you. I was beginning to think I missed some of the ale you tried to smuggle on board."

Slogar feigned insult, "Who me? Why, I would never stoop to such a level as to have a secondary stash of ale. Only because I didn't think of it, mind you. The truth, I'm sad to say, is that I am as sober as an Elder." Cam suspected that the only reason this was true was the old reprobate couldn't figure out how to get into the ship's store and 'borrow' a bottle.

Instead of putting words to his doubts, he said, "I'm glad to hear that, Slo. Now tell me what you've been doing." Slogar waved his arm to the L-shaped table in the corner of his study, which was really just the far side of the sitting room.

"I've been researching the symptoms that are particular to the epidemic on Creedor. There are several ancient diseases that could be behind them. But my money's on a neuroinvasive virus, most probably rabies."

Exasperated, Cam asked, "Rabbis? I thought rabbis were ancient holy men. How can they be the source of this awful epidemic?"

"Not rabbis, rabies; you know, like babies. You know, Commander, for a smart man, your knowledge of history is pathetic."

Cam indignantly replied, "I know all the military history there is to know. Can I help it if ancient diseases weren't covered?"

"Well, they should have been. Didn't you study Adolph Hitler or Saddam Hussein from twentieth century Earth? Both of these despots used biological warfare to control their own and to destroy their enemies."

"Yes, Slo, I did study them, but bio warfare was mentioned, not expounded upon. But it doesn't matter what I do or don't know about ancient maladies; it does, however, matter what you know. So, what have you learned?"

Slogar sat down by his pseudo-fireplace, balanced his readers on his nose and motioned Cam to sit. He had rejected the notion of corrective surgery for his vision. There was something soothing about having the familiar old vision aid instead.

Taking the chair beside Slogar at the table, Cam waited. "The Emperor tasked his scientific researchers with finding a way to eliminate all diseases among the Empire's citizens. So they set about a long and laborious journey that led them to genetically engineering antidotes that eventually wiped out all diseases — among the people. But what the Emperor and his researchers failed to consider was that some of the most horrendous ailments spring not from man, but from animals. Diseases like rabies, eastern equine encephalitis, Lyme disease, to name just a few, were totally overlooked. Over time, pharmaceutical companies stopped producing antidotes other than those that had been designed through the disease eradication project. As cities grew, wild animal habitats dwindled, driving the poor beasts farther and farther from man but into areas too small to support them. They should have been driven to raid man's cities for food, but they didn't. Why do you think that is, Cam?"

Cam had sat silently, listening intensely to what the doctor was saying. "I never really thought of it, Slo. Where is the area they've been relegated to? Has anyone tried to assess their condition there?"

"As a matter of fact," Slogar expounded, "some covert animal studies have been done. Covert, mind you, because the Emperor doesn't think that the lower animals, other than tredon herds, have a place in our world. What they didn't find was more interesting than what was there. It stands to reason that with these animals having been pushed into the woodlands to the east that among their numbers would be sick animals. They found that all the animals were healthy, which is not possible unless ..."

"Unless someone was harvesting the sick ones. But why would anyone harvest the sick and leave the healthy? Did they leave the carcasses unburied?"

"That's the other thing," the doctor said, "there were no carcasses, no sign that any had been buried. They were just gone. Vanished."

Cam pondered this for a bit, "Doctor, do you think that the intruders harvested the sick animals to generate bio weapons from the animal diseases?"

"That's exactly what I think, Camdus. I only hope that once we've identified the cause of the symptoms, we can access what is needed for an antidote. If it's rabies, a post-exposure prophylaxis can be administered to save the patients. But we will need to capture some of the live virus to formulate a vaccine like the one they used on Earth. Seelah helped me to formulate many antidotes and gave me formulas for many more. But we didn't think of rabies. If it turns out to be rabies, I will need to go back to her home; I can't do this without her." Camdus didn't see how he could let Slogar make this journey and said so.

"Cam, if we bring the Elder Woman here, she loses her powers. Besides, you can't transport her entire lab here. It is extensive."

Cam sighed, "Well, we'll just have to deal with that if or when it becomes necessary. Right now, I need to go check in with my men on the bridge. I'll make sure you have a lab to work in once we get to Creedor, Doctor." Cam heard the swooshing of Slogar's door as it closed behind him. Once in the passageway, he strode swiftly to see how soon they'd be in orbit around Creedor.

Willem Camdus visits Tomer Arking

When Willem got to Capitol City, he checked into a lo-
cal hostel that was known for its discretion. He figured that
he should keep a low profile while here - just in case. In
case of what, he still didn't know. He registered under his
real name but was given a temporary identity. The Emperor
hated hostels like this one, but with its security so sophisti-
cated, Empire Guardsmen were unable to actually identify
which ones were part of the network. Willem had learned
of their existence as a young soldier in the covert ops corps
under old Admiral Grunden. This was one of the few pluses
to the years of separation he had endured away from Rose in
the early part of their life together. He had found this hostel
network that allowed him to disappear while remaining in
plain sight.

After a few moments in the identity protection chamber,
which doubled as a closet, Willem emerged a new man. Literally. Instead of being a wrinkled, middle aged man with
graying hair, he now appeared to be a robust gentleman of
about 30 years. He appraised himself in the full-length mirror. 'Hmmm. I wish Rose could see me now. But I don't
know what's going on here, so it's best to keep her in the
dark awhile longer.' Willem nodded appreciatively to the
inn keeper and stepped out into the briskly paced pedestrian
traffic flowing both ways along the moving sidewalk. He
passed by several men he had served with in the military,
without being recognized. Now his challenge would be to
get in to see Tomer Arking. He He knew he was taking a risk
by using his old identity, but he had to give Tomer a chance
to prove he was innocent of what Michael thought he was
doing. He quickly arrived at the vast office building where
Tomer worked. Checking the directory briefly, he realized
that Tomer was still in the same office. He signed in with

the lobby receptionist using his new identify. The young girl was so struck by this handsome man standing before her that she simply smiled and handed him a visitor's pass. The lift stopped on the 18th floor of the building.

Willem strode purposefully to Tomer's office suite. He was greeted by a much older receptionist, a Miss Stewling by her name plate. "I'd like to see Elder Arking, if that's possible. I'm in town on business and need to speak to him privately while I'm here."

"Do you have an appointment, Mr. . . , Mr. . . , I'm sorry I didn't get your name." "Radfield. Zachary Radfield." He told her he did not have an appointment. The name he had given her was the code name that he had used when he and Tomer were in covert ops together. He prayed Tomer would remember it, only if he were still the Tomer he served with. Otherwise, he was putting himself in terrible danger.

The receptionist touched a button and spoke into the air, "Elder Arking, a Mr. Zachary Radfield is here to see you. He doesn't have an appointment. Would you like me to schedule him one?"

Tomer's unmistakable voice floated back, again seemingly from nowhere. "Of course I'll see Mr. Radfield, Ms. Stewling. Please show him in." The receptionist did as asked and ushered Willem into Tomer's office. With a prudish look, she firmly closed the door on her way out.

When Tomer was quite sure it was safe to speak, he said in a low voice, "Will, my friend. It's been too long. Do have a seat. How is Rose? Pretty as ever, I imagine."

"She is that, Tomer. We're fine, enjoying retirement. We're putterers, you know." Both men laughed at that.

The tone became somber when Tomer asked, "Why the disguise, Will? What's going on?"

"I was hoping you could tell me, Tomer. Surely you have an assistant other than Ms. Stewling?"

"Yes, of course I do. You know that I couldn't possibly perform all my duties without one. Especially now that I have been placed over Diplomatic Affairs and certain classified military missions."

Willem looked at his old friend very hard. How much should he tell him? How much could he trust him? "Tomer, some very disturbing rumors are being spread about you in certain circles. I need to know the truth."

Tomer looked equally hard at Willem. It was hard to take in that this 30 something young man sitting across from him was in fact his own contemporary. Had he not recognized the code name and then the voice, he would've had him removed from the building and delivered to the guards. "What kind of rumors?" Willem quickly filled him in, speaking very softly so as not to be overheard by an overly curious receptionist. "But that's absurd! I've had no such reports. And I am quite confident that Matt Enright would have told me if there were any."

Willem detected an unpleasant mix of emotions in his old friend's voice. Understandable, though. "Tomer, how long has Enright worked for you?"

"Two years now. He came to me from the Empire Intelligence Agency on the best of recommendations." Willem could see that even though Tomer was defending Enright, questions were already forming. He decided that talking further here was too dangerous and invited Tomer to the hostel later in the evening. He thanked Ms. Stewling for her courtesy and rode the lift down. The young girl in the lobby nearly fell out of her chair watching him go. Willem could only chuckle to himself as he caught a glimpse of her out of the corner of his eye. If she only knew. 'Ah, sweet Rose.' He already missed her.

Just after dark, someone knocked at Willem's door. "Who is it?"

"Lenwood Styles." Willem recognized the code name and the voice. He rose from the desk and let Tomer in.

"Well, you transformed nicely yourself, old man," noted Willem. "How does it feel to have a full head of hair again?"

"About as well for me as for you, I imagine," Tomer replied with a chuckle. Willem offered him a seat at the small table and poured them both a stiff drink. Tomer couldn't believe it – Irish whiskey that must be hundreds of years old. And it still had that smooth fire he'd always enjoyed.

"Where did you get this, Will? It's like the nectar of the gods."

"My ancestors actually had a distillery in Ireland back on Earth for centuries. Rose and I have cases of it in the basement beneath our store, though we only open a bottle for very special events. I'm afraid today may mark the beginning of a string of special events, most of them we'll probably regret." Tomer and Willem sipped their whiskey with the perfectly prepared tredon steaks that Will had ordered before Tomer arrived. Savoring the whiskey and fine meal, they talked into the night. By morning, both knew what they had to do. Willem would go back to his home and contact Cam to let him know what he'd learned. Tomer had to find a way to use Enright, if possible, now that he knew he was in league with an unknown enemy. The way ahead was dangerous, but necessary. He longed for the day he could lay his old bald head on his pillow and no longer worry about the Empire he loved so much.

The Real Mission Begins

Grunden decided to check in with Dr. Slogar before returning to his quarters; Slogar had shooed him away earlier. Now Grunden wanted to let him know that he had been assigned as his assistant. He also wanted to make sure the old doctor knew how to access all the features found in his room. He tapped on the door. No answer. He tapped again, louder this time, "Doctor. Dr. Slogar, are you there?" He listened carefully; then he heard the familiar wheezing. The door slid open.

"Good evening, Mr. Grunden. How can I help you?" Grunden asked to come in; Slogar moved heavily aside and gestured to a small seating area. Grunden waited for the doctor to sit before seating himself.

"Doctor, Commander Camdus has assigned me to be your assistant. My quarters are right next door, if you need me. This is the intercom; just push OQ4. See right here. Even if I'm not in my quarters, I'll still be paged with this remote communicator I carry at all times. So I'll be available whenever you need me. And you don't have to get up to answer the door. Once we voice train the computer, just say, 'Enter' from anywhere in the room. The door will open. But always check this monitor before you allow anyone in."

Slogar thought, 'Well, at least that explained why every time I've tried to use the "enter" command, the confounded door refused to obey.' For some moments Slogar studied the soldier, for that seemed to be the best description of Grunden. It seemed that he was to have a body guard, whether he wanted one or not. He sighed. If he were really honest with himself, he knew he needed one; he had long since lost the ability to fight or to run. 'May as well be gracious,' he mused.

"Well, Mr. Grunden. I welcome your help. I just hope that you won't find this assignment too boring." Somehow Grunden doubted anything that happened on board the ship or on Creedor would be boring. That would be wishful thinking.

"Thank you, Dr. Slogar. Now, let me help familiarize you with your new home. Doctor, to have full access to your quarters' features you need to 'train' the voice activated computer which controls the door, intercom, nutrition center, as well as its entertainment features and library archives. So if you'll be so kind — please speak to your computerized control center so that it will recognize your voice and will be able to respond to you." Slogar complied. "Thank you, Doctor. Now, please allow me to show you to your launch chair."

As Grunden demonstrated the launch chair, Slogar asked, "Mr. Grunden, who else on the ship is authorized to enter these quarters?"

Now it was Grunden who studied the doctor for a brief moment. "Since you have taken over the voice control of this unit, only you, the Commander, Captain Slag, and of course, me. And unless you give us permission, we can only enter when the control senses that you are either in need of assistance or are no longer viable."

Slogar thought about this for a moment. "You mean, that if I'm sick or dead, you can enter. No other time, without an invitation. Right?"

"That's correct, Sir. Now if you'll excuse me, I have to be report to my station. Good evening, Doctor. Please remember to secure yourself in your launch chair whenever an alert is sounded. I'll come back at your summons, after we attain Creedorian orbit." With that, Grunden left Slogar, who was busy practicing strapping himself into and releasing himself from his launch chair. Grunden noted as he walked down the corridor to his station that the doctor had not let the little bag out of his reach the entire time he'd been there. 'It doesn't look like much, but whatever's in it must be pretty important,' he thought as he reached his destination. He figured he better make sure that he helped the doctor keep it safe, just in case.

Captain Slag was at the helm with Commander Camdus by his side. The Captain was somewhat of a maverick as captains in the service went. He had been down ranked from admiral to captain after losing the Empire's number one fighting cruiser in what should have been a routine flight over what was charted as an uninhabited planet in the Troglite solar system. He had managed to evacuate the crew in the transpods but unlike most officers in command, refused to go down with his ship. He used the mini pod for his own escape when he realized that nothing he could do would salvage the ship. He saw nothing heroic in giving his life for a piece of equipment. Slag liked chilled wine and warm women and a good month's pay. His philosophy had always been, "There's no future in dying." Slag had not asked to be made admiral, anyway. But he had tried to do the right thing. The ship on which he was flying as guest dignitary came under fire from an unknown source; the young captain panicked. Slag had no other choice of action. He had taken command from the wet-behind-the-ears captain and flown the hell out of that ship as long as she had any life left in her. If he hadn't been outnumbered, he had no doubt that he would have brought an undamaged ship home. He thought he had done about as well as anyone could have under the circumstances, but Reglon Empire Guard was not pleased.

Not only did he lose his admiralty, he was reassigned to the nearest thing to a garbage scow in the fleet. When he first came aboard, the damn thing would barely respond to any commands it was so rusty. And its weapons systems were obsolete. Slag had sat back and studied his situation. 'I will not let them whip me on this.' He rallied some of his former crewmen who managed to get assigned to his quadrant. They began furtively working on the ship to update its weapons and give it a power booster. In retrospect, Slag realized that what he had now was the perfect warship. It looked like a rust bucket ready to be scrapped, but it ran like the well-tuned, heavily armed precision machine it had become. And nowhere in Reglon Empire Guard records was any trace of its modifications. This meant that nothing could be leaked to any mole that might have infiltrated the Emperor's ranks. What he had was a secret weapon just waiting for a call to service. It was Commander Michael Camdus who had made that call.

"We have orbit, Commander. We're ready to release the shuttlecraft on your order," Captain Slag reported. Camdus looked out the port viewer to see the endless blanket of black studded with stars and space debris. Looking down he saw the brown ball with tiny green specks that was the planet Creedor. It looked hazy from this altitude due to the hellish winds whipping its natural sand surface. If one looked long enough, it seemed to change shape, almost as if it were alive and breathing. Camdus shuddered at the thought of returning to its surface. Prolonging the mission would only make it worse, he knew, yet his sense of dread grew minute by minute.

He responded to Slag, "Order the shuttles loaded with all the supplies they'll hold. We will make as many trips as necessary to complete the transfer. Contact Base C Leader and secure permission to transport all cargo. Let me know when this has been done so that we can begin transporting passengers and crew. I will be in my quarters until time for our departure. Captain."

The Tonlin Cottage

The silence around Mara was unbearable. She had been in hiding for what seemed like an eternity and still Ramar had not come for her. She listened so intently that she could hear her own heart beating loudly in her ears. Ram had sent her into hiding days ago; she was not sure how many. Why had he not come for her? Verging on panic, Mara carefully slid the panel as quietly as she could. When she had an opening large enough to allow sound to pass, she held her breath so that she could detect the slightest noise. She heard the wind whipping; it sounded as if it were raging through her house. But Ram would never have opened the door during demon wind season unless he had to check on the livestock, especially when he was on guard against the intruders. She knew he had just checked the livestock before he sent her into hiding. Now more afraid for Ramar than herself, Mara left her hiding place, being careful to replace the panel as it was before. From the closet she peeked out into the bedroom.

Everything was topsy turvy, their clothes strewn, shutters torn from the windows, and the picture of Astril was smashed against the wall. When she saw that, Mara just knew that Ram was dead. He would have to be, to allow anyone to touch Astril's picture. She ran to the kitchen, fearing what she felt sure she would find. The kitchen door was open, sand swirling in mini-dunes across her floor. Ramar was nowhere to be found. Covering her face with a scarf, Mara ran to the livestock shelter. All the animals had been slaughtered and left to rot. She searched the shelter and its adjoining feed room. Ram's nucleo-laser was lying on the floor in the corner. There was blood on the handle. Yellow blood. He had wounded one of them, but they had taken him. How could they have taken the only person she had left on Creedor. The panic rose in her chest. She would never see him again. In addition to losing their daughter, she and Ram had also lost all their friends to either the intruders or the epidemic. Why couldn't they have taken her, too? She recalled the roaring argument that she and Ram had about their plan if they were attacked by the intruders. Ram had totally refused to go into hiding with her, convinced that he would be able to stop them. He had laid an elaborate set of traps on the perimeter of the walking yard and at strategic places in the outer areas as well. Any who managed to get through would be eliminated with his nucleo-laser. She had scorned this as paltry in the face of such powerful enemies. Now she wished that she had been wrong.

Once back inside the cottage, she closed the door and barred it. Overcome by what had happened, Mara slid to the floor and sobbed until there were no tears left. Yet she felt no relief from the ache in her chest. She sat amid the sand dunes in her kitchen and began to feel angry. How dare they destroy everything and everyone in her world! And just who in the hell were they anyway? Ram and Mara had settled on Creedor when their home planet of Vartuch had been so irreversibly polluted that the environment became unbearable. The beautiful green pastures and forests had become wastelands. The once clear sky was now so hazy from toxic fumes that it would literally disintegrate the fabric of the pedestrian's outer clothing. Children were going blind from exposure to the hazardous chemicals found in their drinking water. Mobile craft of all designs were banned and there was no energy to fuel even the lights, much less the appliances. In the forced blackouts, crime thrived. Living on Vartuch had become such a nightmare that Ram and Mara had sought jobs on some other planet whose environment was tolerable, though none had the beauty that Vartuch once had. After several months, Mara had secured a job as a mineral technician on Creedor, a planet rich with iron ore as well as gold and, even more valuable, trizactl. Ram had not been able to get a job right away and was encouraged by Mara to take this opportunity to raise a herd of tredons like he had always wanted to do. Tredons were hardy stock that had a market Empire-wide. All he had to do was get a good herd established, build a good reputation, and he would never have to work for anyone else again. Mara had been so proud of him when he bought his first cow and bull. It was as if he were a father again. Astril was two then and loved to follow her father around the stockyard as he tended the animals. She had given pet names to them, even though Ram had tried to get her to understand that they could not keep them for always. Ram tasted success when he sold the first calf for enough to buy another cow and feed for all three animals for the winter. Bossy and Maude, as Astril dubbed the cows, were very fertile and each produced a calf the following spring. With the proceeds from the sale of one of the calves, he had bought Mara a carriage for her horse so that she would not have to walk to her lab anymore. Mobile craft that burned fossil fuel had been banned on Creedor more than 200 years ago. The environment had in some respects rejuvenated itself, but the legacy left by their forefathers was so great that no one dared to suggest that mobile craft be reinstated. The only craft allowed to operate on Creedor were the Reglon Empire Guard cruisers and pods which emitted no noxious fumes. This restricted use of mobile craft was good for the environment, but made it hard for others to get around. No one could legally own them as personal vehicles, not even Emperor Jarlod, though he and his cronies regularly broke this law.

Mara finally got up and looked out the window again; it was already dark outside. Though she had only eaten tiny portions of the emergency supplies while in hiding, she had no desire to eat. But the house was getting cold and the howling had started again. She built a small fire for warmth and heated water for tea. As she nailed the broken shutters back over the windows, she thought how stupid it all was. If the intruders didn't get her, either the epidemic or some crazed epidemic victim would. That is, if she did not starve to death first. It was too dangerous to try to save any of the meat from the slain animals. Who knew what contaminants they had been exposed to from the intruders or how long she might have without fear of being discovered by Lord only knew what kinds of twisted relics of humanity the epidemic had produced. She finished her task of securing the cottage again physically exhausted and emotionally wrung. Collapsing on her bed, Mara could smell Ram's own special scent on his pillow. She had always thought that he smelled just like sunshine. Holding his pillow to her, she fell into a fitful sleep.

Demon Winds

"There, Commander. I see a house sitting next to the edge of that plateau. It looks as if it's abandoned. There are no lights, and no . . . Wait! There's a wisp of smoke coming from the chimney. Either someone is home or has been recently. Shall we land amid the dunes just south of there?" The shuttle pilot had reservations about the Captain and Commander's orders to steer clear of Clandil, the capital city of Creedor. He knew that was where the epidemic was at its worst, so why didn't his commanding officers want to go there first. Their mission was, after all, to discover some way to at least control the spread of the epidemic even if they could not stop it. At least that was the scuttlebutt among the crew.

Captain Slag gave permission to land on the plateau as the pilot had suggested. "Steady, Mr. Cronwell. We don't want to lose the craft to those winds. Try to find a lea just beyond the dwelling. That should shield us from the wind currents enough to land safely." Cronwell deftly maneuvered the shuttle to the location indicated. As he was lowering the landing stilts, a gust caught the craft and bounced it as if it were a kite.

"Damn it, Cronwell. Give me that control!" Slag took the helm and righted the craft within seconds of a disastrous crash. Cronwell could only look on amazed at the easy, sure-handed way the Captain regained stability and in the process saved the ship and their skins. He had just witnessed what had become legend among the Fleet. As a cadet he had heard about the daring and skill of Captain Slag, but as all cadets before and since, none believed that Slag was anything more than an egotistical blowhard who had lucked out on some mission or other and impressed the brass. When he was busted, the cadets felt that they had been right. After all, it took a real screw-up to lose an admiralty. Captain Slag completed the landing maneuver without a word. When everyone else had left the craft, he called Cronwell to him. "You didn't have the auxiliary stabilizers engaged. That was stupid. I don't like stupid mistakes. Do you understand, Mr. Cronwell, or do I have to quote Fleet Code to you?" Cronwell knew the Code very well. And he sure as hell did not want to face a Command Inquiry into the question of his competence.

"Captain Slag, Sir. I made an error in judgment. I misjudged the pattern of the wind current and the strength of the wind shear. I acknowledge my negligence and am fully prepared to be relieved of duty."

"Cronwell, right now we can't spare you for disciplinary action. Perhaps you should give serious thought to what you should have done today, what you didn't do, and what the consequences would have been had I not been here. Until further notice, you are barred from the bridge of the mother cruiser. When this is over, Commander Camdus may well want to implement additional disciplinary measures your infraction merits. But know this; if you ever make this mistake again, I will personally recommend the inquiry for you. Do you understand, Mister?"

"Very clearly, Sir."

"Good. Take your place with the landing party and begin the search of the plateau for any, I repeat, any humans. Dismissed."

Captain Slag didn't use the threat of the inquiry lightly; he still remembered his own vividly. Yes, he had lived through it, but it had left its indelible mark seared into his psyche. That he was still sane was amazing after the torturous inter-rogation he had been subjected to. No one in the Fleet spoke of the event anymore. Even when the ordeal was underway, it was only mentioned by those inexperienced pilots and ca-dets who had never known anyone who had been through it. Though the inquiry was held behind barred doors with only authorized personnel present, there were inevitable leaks of the inhumane treatment and torture of Slag and the threats to his family, which caused him a deeper, more permanent pain. He would never forget - ever. Most who underwent the inquiry broke after only a few hours, signing an admission of guilt or negligence, as the case may be, and accepting their term in the military prison on Vuthral with something akin to joy. Victor Slag had not broken. Not when they brought in his wife and son and forced him to watch as they brutally interrogated them as if they were criminals. Not even when his wife Janara begged their tormentors to have pity on the boy and spare him. Victor had felt as if his heart was being squeezed by a huge fist, yet he made not one sound. The insanity of this farce called an "inquiry" was not nearly as in-sane as the premise that he had conspired with the enemy, whoever the hell they were, to systematically sabotage all the Fleet super cruisers. In time, he had been exonerated, but he had been forever changed. The silent oath of vengeance he had taken that day is what kept him going.

Slogar meets Mrs. Tonlin

The sound of voices woke Mara from her troubled sleep. It was dark out now, so she couldn't tell if it was the intruders returning or villagers seeking some poor demented soul to put of his misery. Either way, she needed to be cautious. Slipping from the bed to the floor without making a sound, Mara edged her way to the window facing the walking yard. Through the slats of the shutters, she could see the light from a lamp of some sort coming from the direction of the animal stalls. She held her breath hoping to hear better.

"Dr. Slogar, be careful. There appear to be booby traps around the perimeter of this property. Whoever lives or used to live here must have been expecting trouble. Here, let me take your bag." Grunden reached to take Slogar's bag, which seemed to be throwing the doctor off balance, only to have it snatched from his grasp.

"That won't be necessary, Mr. Grunden. I am quite capable of ... Ooof!" Slogar stepped into a soft drift of sand, lost his balance entirely, and fell flat on his round belly. Grunden, much taller and stronger, floundered after him with his light and dragged the doctor roughly to his feet.

"Listen, Dr. Slogar. If we're going to work together, you are going to have to trust me sooner or later. So you may as well start now or we may both find ourselves buried in this miserable sand. Now, give me that bag and take my arm so I can get us out of here. Let's head for the back of the dwelling. Maybe we can get inside and out of this dismal wind."

"You make a good point, Grunden, but you must give me your word on your honorable mother's head that you will protect this bag with your life if need be."

Grunden heaved the doctor to a halt. "Wait just a minute. I want to know what's in that bag if I may have to die for it. So, tell me, Doctor. What is it you're asking me to risk my life for?"

"Get us out of this windstorm, Mr. Grunden. When you need to know, I'll brief you on everything. But I must get out of this accursed sand! I'm beginning to feel as if I'm going to suffocate any minute." Slogar was wheezing louder now and Grunden could feel the fear rising within his charge, though the darkness shielded his face.

"Okay, Doctor," Grunden reassured, "we're almost there. Just a couple more steps. Here. Now if I can just jimmy this door."

Mara held her breath as she flattened herself inside the closet of her bedroom. She wanted to get a look at these men before she barricaded herself in her hiding place. She heard someone at the back door and a second later it opened with such force that it slammed into the wall. She heard the men as they made their way inside. One of them was having difficulty breathing. She could hear them talking but couldn't distinguish what they were saying. 'Maybe one of them is sick. Oh, Lord. Maybe it's an epidemic victim being brought here for isolation. I'm sure the place must look deserted.' Suddenly she saw one of them enter her bedchamber. Though his lamplight was dim, she let out a sigh of relief when she saw the Reglon Empire Guard emblem on his uniform: indigo REG letters written across seven golden circles overlapping into one. Mara burst from the closet so abruptly that Grunden pulled his weapon and took aim, ready to shoot.

"Halt. I am a Reglon Empire Guard soldier and am fully prepared to neutralize you where you stand." When he detected that the enemy had halted, he approached with his lamp in one hand, his weapon still at the ready in the other.

"Don't shoot! I am unarmed. This is my home that you have broken into, and I have never been so glad for anything in my life. Please put your weapon down. I need help finding my husband. They took him and I don't know where to look for him. They are all gone. Everyone that I loved has been destroyed on this world. I wish I had never heard of it." Mara had reached a near hysterical pitch, but the reality of what she just said sucked the breath from her; she felt the room spinning as she lost consciousness.

Grunden reacted in a split second, dropped the lamp and swept the woman up just before she hit the floor, saving her from cracking her head like an egg on the rough stone. "Doctor, I need you in here, now," he called over his shoulder. Slogar had by this time regained his breath. He went as quickly as his lumbering body could manage to see what Grunden had found. The sight of this small, blonde woman surprised him. Why would she be here alone? It was obviously a very dangerous location, so isolated on this sand strewn plateau.

"Well, Mr. Grunden. Who is this? Surely, this little slip of a girl is no threat to a big, strong soldier. Put that weapon down. You'll scare her to death when she comes to." Grunden holstered his side arm, but kept his hand close to it. Women were warriors, too. He'd learned that from one of his first skirmishes as a young soldier. Slogar approached Mara and patted her hand gently to try to wake her. She woke with a jolt, startled to see these two strange men in her bedchamber.

"My name is Simon Slogar, my dear. I am a physician. This rather brusque gentleman is my very able assistant, Mr. Grunden. We are with Reglon Empire Guard's Special Research Team. We are trying to determine the cause of the epidemic that is plaguing Creedor and then to find some way to stop it. I am terribly sorry if we frightened you." Slogar's patient, fatherly manner seemed to put Mara at ease. He patted her hand again and said, "Now, Miss, please tell us why you're living here all alone."

Ramar Enslaved

When Ramar woke up, he found himself lying on the hot, stone floor of a cave. Though dimly lit, he could make out the forms of other creatures nearby. Like Ramar, all were in shackles. At the mouth of the cave were two well-armed guards. From the look of them, they were of the asteroid colony Trotin, probably from the Translavan region, known allies of the Q'Arons. Ramar wondered what they were doing on Creedor. Yes, he was still on Creedor. Where exactly, he was not sure. But he guessed that he was in some portion of a trizactl mine, most likely the one breached by intruders not two months before.

The news release from Emperor Jarlod misrepresented the entire affair, referring to an inadvertent straying from course by a ship from a neighboring world. He omitted the fact that these were Q'Arons. And he either didn't know or decided to ignore the part about a contingent leaving the ship and actually entering the mines. The report should have been a huge alarm sounding throughout the Empire. Instead it was a whimper, heard by no one. After all, the two Empires had been enemies since the beginning of the Jarlod reign because of a dispute over the planet Creedor's vast store of trizactl, a mineral both empires needed for the production of power for homes, and for nucleo-laser weapons and shields. The Q'Arons maintained that it was unfair for the Empire to have sole control of such a potentially deadly mineral, especially when they did not have matching fire power. Jarlod would not listen to any arguments for a peaceful disarmament, or even a reduction in the rate at which the Empire's stockpile was being increased. He seemed possessed by the thought that the more lethal weapons he had, the better the chances of keeping peace. He was intractable, though many of the Empire's most brilliant philosophers and strategists tried to reason with him about the danger of continuing his weapons build up. After a time, he became tired of listening to his advisors and instead of negotiating, Jarlod declared sanctions against the Q'Aron Empire that prohibited any of its citizens, military or civilian, from setting foot on Creedor. He further made it illegal for any Creedorian to communicate with any Q'Aron on any matter. The penalty for breaking this law was death by space implosion, a brutal but instant demise.

In spite of all the Emperor's best efforts to preserve what he deemed as his, the enemy had scored a huge victory. What the Emperor didn't know was that the intruders had not been routed as he had thought. The Q'Arons had merely planted their own engineers within the Reglon mine and lasered their way from there to the massive trizactl deposit several miles away. Jarlod didn't even know this deposit existed. It would have required him to consider the fact that the existing supply would someday be exhausted for him to even consider looking for other deposits. This error in judgment was one of his most damaging.

Ramar and the others had no knowledge of the politics involved in their current predicament. It wouldn't have mattered if they had. They could only try to survive, one hour at a time. Ram was a little disoriented at first. Thankfully, except for a few cuts and bruises, he was unharmed. Aside from being held prisoner, his biggest discomfort was the pounding headache. He licked his parched lips; they were cracked and bleeding from thirst. As he squinted into his dim surroundings, he became aware that the others had stiffened and all but one had ceased making any sounds.

From the far corner the same raspy breathing that must have been there all the time finally caught his attention. He found that he could move about, though the shackles on his wrists and ankles made getting on his feet very difficult. Once he was upright, he tried to get a sense of his surroundings. The moaning in the corner was weaker now. Ramar could feel the tension among his fellow prisoners as he moved closer to sound, yet no one spoke. Just as he reached his destination, a hand as rough as pure emery seized his wrist. Startled, Ramar jerked around to face whoever it was that held him in such an iron grip.

"Leave him alone," the man rasped too close to Ram's face. "He can't help us anymore. He tried, but he was no match for them. Now we have to watch him die in this God-forsaken place." The man's hot, stale breath assaulted Ramar's nostrils.

Ram leaned close to the man's ear and whispered, "But who are you, and why are you here? And how could . . . ."

"You don't know what happens to us here. If they catch us talking, we will be taken to Lars' room for his 'amusement.' Shhhh. Get back in line; they're coming." The man pulled Ramar back into the ranks of the others.

"Well, let's see what we have in this cave. The others have been no sport at all. What filthy beasts! Too bad they can't be disinfected and deodorized before I have to make my selection. I think I'll tell Daddy that he must do that or I positively refuse to choose from them. I don't know why I can't have one of the soldiers anyway. They are younger and smell nicer. You wouldn't mind that, would you, Lt. T'Aron?" The woman was apparently speaking to the tall man walking beside her as they entered the cave. Ramar made note of the four as they approached. They were led by an old man who appeared quite feeble followed the tall soldier, who Ramar guessed was Lt. T'Aron, and a young woman whose petulance was evident in her voice. A heavily armed guard brought up the rear. As the woman approached, Ram could smell her scent and hear the rustle of her silk. Though he could not see very well in the dimly lit cave, the light of the old man's torch illuminated his weathered face and hand. On his gnarled index finger rested a ring with a large fiery stone flanked by two rubies set in serpentine gold. The light shifted when the old man held the torch higher; its light bathed the woman's face. It was framed by raven black hair so shiny that it reflected the light of the torch; her eyes glittered like huge dark pearls beneath what he thought had to be phony eyelashes. Ramar had never seen a woman like this before. The memory of Mara's pale beauty flashed across his mind as if to enunciate the stark difference between the two women. A pang of guilt and sorrow struck him so deeply and swiftly as he involuntarily remembered that he had left Mara in the hiding place, not knowing whether they had found her and silently praying that they had not. He wished now he had listened to her when she tried to dissuade him from his plan.

A hand on his bare chest brought Ram back to reality as he became instantly rigid, fearful that he was to be taken to Lars, whoever that was, as the other prisoner had warned him. The woman was staring him full in the face. "Hmm, this one is young, and strong. Just feel these muscles." Ramar felt another, harsher touch. He held his breath. "I'll take this one. What's that horrid sound? Slafe, bring the torch."

The old man cast the light from the torch in the direction indicated by the woman. It illuminated an ancient looking man crumpled in a heap on the floor in the cave's corner. Ramar gasped as he recognized his friend Stadar, whom he had assumed was dead when Stadar had disappeared during the first intruder invasion. Stadar now looked like a poor old grandfather, though Ramar knew Stad was only a few years older than he. What had happened to him? Involuntarily he made as if to move toward Stadar, only to be yanked back into line by his unknown comrade. Lt. T'Aron took one long stride and was standing in front of Ram looking intently at him, weapon at the ready. Ram stood stock still, hoping that he had not perceived his recognition of his old friend, for instinct told him that this knowledge would mean more bad news. Just at that moment, the woman summoned the guard to raise the old man to his feet. Ram silently breathed his relief as the soldier stepped aside to allow the guard to pass so as to obey the woman.

Once on his feet, Stadar was closely scrutinized by the woman. It was almost as if she were trying to see into his mind, to read his thoughts. Ram could see the beads of sweat pouring profusely from underneath Stad's shaggy hair, down his deeply lined, grimy face into his filthy beard. He could see why the others thought that Stadar was old; had he not recognized the distinct shamrock shaped birthmark on Stadar's right cheek, Ram would not have known him, either.

"Well, well. The old one seems to have nothing on his mind except his friend Humpty Dumpty. I will make you a promise, Old Man. Humpty won't be the only one that can't be put back together again if you try anything else." She continued to study him. "Have you lost your wits in the service of His Majesty's Master Slaver? Or perhaps you don't want anyone to know what is what is truly on your mind. A few more days and you won't matter — if you're still alive."

Then she addressed her party, "We'll keep him here just to be sure that he doesn't get any more bright ideas like the insurrection he tried to start when he first arrived. My, my, how I hated to watch Lars turn you into such a decrepit old man. You were such a strong, stubborn specimen. Did you know that the whip actually fell from Lars' grip he was so tired from his session with you? And now to find you a babbling fool. Lars will be pleased to know his work was not in vain. Release him. He will not be planning any more escapes." Stadar fell heavily to the floor. When his raspy breath momentarily ceased, Ramar feared him dead but had no time to worry about his friend as he himself was almost instantly jerked forward by his chained wrists and shoved along before Lt. T'Aron down a long dark hall until he was soon outside the cave. For the first time, Ramar saw his surroundings. Spread before him was an immense underground fortress. All around its perimeter were guard towers equipped with nucleo cannons. He estimated that each one had the ability to destroy a small village with one volley. He wondered what the Q'Arons intended to do with this installation. He knew that whatever it was, it spelled catastrophe for the Empire since the Q'Arons were not supposed to be here at all. He also wondered how they were able to build such a place without someone high up in the Empire having knowledge of its existence. These ponderings led him to some very unsettling conclusions that he would have been better not to think about, at least not so close to the woman who was obviously clairvoyant.

He recognized her scent, so he knew she was near. In an instant she sidled up to him. She spoke to him in a voice that sounded like a contented cat purring. "It is easy to read your discontent. It is also easy to read you past connections with Stadar, innocent though they may have been. If you are wise, and I do hope that you will be wiser than he was, you will forget Stadar and you will cease to wonder about this place. Since there is no escape from here other than through death, I shall tell you where you are. The rest you will learn when you have performed to my standards and have earned the privilege of asking questions. Until then, ask none. Do you understand me?" When Ram nodded affirmatively, she continued. "I am Li'Let, daughter of His Majesty's Master Slaver, Thurl. You are, as you so rightly suppose, in the Creedorian mines though not exactly as you envisioned them. This is Q'Door Hold. Its purpose is none of your concern. I am your only concern. Your life depends on how well you play my game. Many have tried, some have succeeded. Your friend Stadar was very good, but could not put aside his futile notion that he could escape and take the other slaves with him. He was a very foolish man. He had a privileged life that he could have kept until I tired of him, which would not have happened for quite some time had he played by the rules. But Stadar is no longer to be your concern. Remember, your survival depends on me. Now, Lt. T'Aron. Take Ramar. That is your name, isn't it? Yes, Ramar. Take Ramar to the spa. I want him in my chamber tonight. Slafe, if you will escort me back I will begin preparations."

Ramar didn't know if what she had in mind was what it sounded like. And he sincerely hoped that it was not. He had been faithful to Mara since the first time he had seen her, even before they had made a commitment to each other.

She was in his heart always. But now that he knew that Li'Let could read minds, Ram would have to mask his thoughts. An ancient nursery rhyme that Stadar had used had stymied Li'Let. He would have to find something equally banal to protect his thoughts. He also knew how blessed he was that Li'Let wasn't trying to read his mind earlier when his mind wandered to Mara. At least he hoped she hadn't. He didn't know how he knew, but he knew that he had to protect Mara from this apparently twisted individual. Though beautiful outwardly, something about this Li'Let made his blood run cold.

A sharp poke in the ribs hastened Ramar on. Cool fresh air engulfed him as he entered the room which, as best he could reckon, was in the northernmost turret. As he looked about him, he saw that the room glowed a soft blue though from what source he could not say. Lt. T'Aron shoved him into a side chamber equipped with a shower that was already running very warm water.

"When I unshackle you, be smart. You can't escape so save us all some time and pain." As soon as he was free, he was told to disrobe and step into the shower. Seeing no future in disobeying his captor, Ramar did as he was told. The water smelled of disinfectant, foaming from the nozzles in huge ropes of spray. Eyes closed against the stringent liquid, Ram could not see who —what — was roughly scrubbing him from head to foot. As quickly as the unseen assistant came, it disappeared. The water was now light and cool, the disinfectant replaced with aromatic essential oils. When the water finally stopped Ram took the huge towel offered him by an attendant, a rather large man whose eyes were definitely out of place.

"You look to be one she'll keep for quite some time, Creedorian ... if you are lucky. Otherwise, you could end up like me, or dead." Ram knew from the man's high pitched voice that he was a eunuch; not a fate he that he wished for himself. Death would be preferable. He was about to ask about Li'Let when Lt. T'Aron re-entered and tossed him a navy blue uniform of a light weight, silken fabric that Ramar had never seen before. Lt. T'Aron ordered him to don the garment. Ram didn't much like the thought of wearing something so flimsy, but noticing that his own clothes were gone, he put it on. Anything to cover his nakedness would do. He was a little relieved when he realized that the uniform was far more substantial than he thought.

"She's waiting for you. Be sure you play the game or we will all suffer. You, most of all." That was the second time T'Aron had hinted that EVERYONE was punished when the Master Slaver's daughter was not pleased. He wanted to ask about the game, but the look on T'Aron's face stopped him. He'd find out soon enough. He couldn't get past the feeling that there was something distinctly odd about this woman Li'Let.

Lt. T'Aron escorted Ramar to Li'Let's chamber which was just below the pinnacle of the turret. T'Aron tapped on the door. From within came Li'Let's velvet invitation to enter. "I bring the slave Ramar, Mistress. Will there be any other requirements of my services this evening?" On receiving a negative reply, Lt. T'Aron took his leave. Ramar could see the sheer anguish in T'Aron's eyes as he left. Perhaps he could turn that to his advantage later. Right now he was faced with his own situation that demanded his full attention so as to remain alive, and masculine, for Mara.

"You know that I can read your mind, don't you? So it would be well if you try to keep your thoughts on me. I do not like to compete with memories. Do you think you can do this?" Li'Let had slowly made her way from her huge, bone-shaped bed and stood some feet away from Ram. She wore a black velvet body suit. Though it was warm in her room, the weird energy that spanned the gap between them sent chills down his spine. He tensed and stepped back. Li'Let's laugh, low and sinister, let Ramar know that he was not the first to try to resist her game. With two long strides, she stood before him. She reached up as if to lovingly touch his cheek. But instead, he felt a sharp pain. The astonished Ram touched his face. Drawing his hand away, he realized she had scratched him so deeply with her claw-like nails that she'd drawn blood. He saw that she was licking her lips. He stepped back, trying to reassess the situation. He had so feared that she wanted intimacy. He knew now that was absolutely NOT what was on her mind. This was crazy; what was this fiend trying to do to him? Just then, the wall behind Li'Let dissolved, revealing a huge maze. Li'Let's laughter was enough to let him know that he had no choice. He took off toward the maze. She stretched like a lazy cat; then she bounded after him.

The maze was both a blessing and a curse, as Li'Let seemed to have supernatural senses. Each turn brought him within a whisper of her. How did she do it? About two-thirds of the way in by his reckoning, Ram saw a small chink in the maze wall. He tried to squeeze his way in, but he was too large. 'Oh Lord, help me,' he silently prayed. He felt himself slide through the opening. He expected to be on the other side of the wall, but found that he was in a very small cavern within the wall. He stood stock still, hardly breathing. He heard someone coming, sure that Li'Let would find him. Outside, something sniffed and snuffled. Then he heard a blood curdling growl; whatever it was raced off. He listened for such a long time that he finally slid down to the floor of the cavern and drifted into fitful slumber. When he awoke, he was back in the cell with the rest of the slaves. He was worn out both physically and mentally, and not a little confused. After a short respite, he was returned to Li'Let's chamber. He wasn't sure what had happened, but he knew that this Li'Let woman, if she was a woman, was not exactly human. What she was, he couldn't say, but she had an incredibly sadistic idea of "play." What he had endured was filled with sheer terror and physical endurance. His faith was still strong, though he couldn't figure out why this was happening to him. So this was the game: try to make it through the maze without being caught. He was convinced that God had answered his prayer, for this woman was truly superhuman. Without God's intervention, he could not have survived. He now had to believe that his fate would not be irrevocably sealed by death or emasculation.

Ramar had something to learn here, so he'd better try to learn it and to do that, he had to survive. First, he had to find a better way to mask his thoughts, to sublimate his innermost fears. He had to be able to endure, to be more challenging prey for Li'Let. Then perhaps she would allow him to begin to ask questions and maybe she would slip with information that could help him get out of here. He knew that he had to try. He heard her soft tread across the deeply plush floor as she returned. His thoughts became a litany of how exciting the game had been and how much he had enjoyed it. The smile on her face let him know that she had read his mind; the look in her eyes told him recess was over. The wall disappeared again, and the game was on.

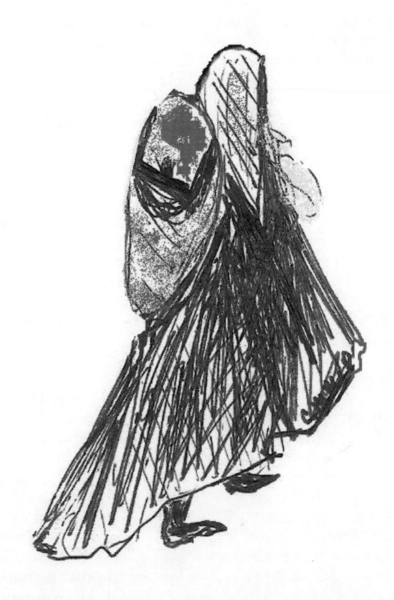

Mara Asks For Help

The heat from the steaming mug seemed to calm Mara as she paused from time to time in telling Slogar and Grunden her story. The thistle tea was strong and conquered the chill Mara had felt since she first realized that Ram was gone. She could see the concern and alarm registering on their faces as she spoke.

"So you see, I have to believe that Ramar is alive. And, I have to find him. The intruders will destroy him, if he isn't rescued soon. I don't know where he is, but I know that there is only one thing on this planet any Empire would find worth fighting over – trizactl. If he hasn't been seriously injured, my guess is he is being used to work the mines. He is young and strong, perfect slave material. Well, almost perfect. He is also an intelligent, independent thinker who has the courage to try to do the right thing. That's what really worries me. He may well do something foolish – brave but still foolish – that might get him killed. I don't think I could take it if anything happened to him. I've lost everyone else in my life – my child, my friends. I won't let them take him, too. Not without a fight, anyway. Please help me; I can't do this alone." Mara's voice was steady despite the tears that streaked her dirt-smudged face. Grunden felt an immense surge of admiration for this little woman. She had indeed lost everything, but instead of steeping in self-pity, she was making plans to either get back what was hers or get even. He liked that in a woman.

Slogar spoke first. "Mara, we are not at liberty to assist you at this moment; we are on an urgent mission that can't wait. If you will remain here until we have completed our task, we will solicit assistance from our Commander and launch an all-out search."

Mara carefully placed the mug on the table, leaned back in her chair, and looked Slogar directly in the eye. "Doctor, I understand your position. Now you need to understand mine. There is no telling what horror Ramar is facing at this very moment. I will NOT wait. I am leaving as soon as possible for the far side of the planet where most of the rogue trizactl mines are probably located. If he is there, I will find him. If he is no more, then nothing they do to me can cause me any greater pain. Good luck on you mission, gentlemen. Now, if you'll excuse me, I have to get ready for my journey." Mara rose from the table.

As she turned to leave the room, Grunden caught her arm. "Mara, wait. Let me contact the Commander. Perhaps he'll give me permission to accompany you. I think your journey may actually help us in our mission. It will take only a few minutes. Will you wait?" Slogar witnessed this exchange with a mixture of amusement and annoyance, but said nothing.

Mara slowly sat back down, acknowledging her willingness to have Grunden's company if allowed. Who knew what lay before her? Grunden looked like a soldier who had seen many battles and definitely would be an asset. She watched as he opened his communicator and raised the Commander. After several exchanges between Grunden and Camdus, it was decided that the Commander would send two of his Special Forces soldiers as escorts for Dr. Slogar and Grunden would accompany Mara, with the strict proviso that Grunden was to check in every four hours using the encrypted code devised especially for this mission. Mara breathed a silent *thank you*. For all her bravado, she was scared of what lay ahead, especially if she had to go it alone.

Dr. Slogar watched as Grunden and Mara set out against the swirling sands. "God be with you both," he prayed softly as he fervently hoped that they reached shelter before nightfall. It wasn't long before they were out of sight and Slogar now quite alone, barred the door and brewed more thistle tea. Once settled in Ram's chair with his tea, he pulled his equipment case to him and snapped it open. A computer the size of a small typewriter from Earth's twentieth century popped into place. Slogar began swiftly querying and rejecting answers at such a rapid pace that he almost missed the link that he had been looking for. The file he had just accessed was a Boldoonian file from the twenty-third century. Most of the terms were archaic, but thanks to Slogar's insatiable curiosity during his early university years, he was familiar with most of them. It seems that the virus that was running rampant on Creedor made its first appearance after the Q'Aron Empire had invaded Boldoon some seven hundred years ago. Only one ship of invaders arrived causing the Reglon Emperor at the time to laugh. However, within a short time the Boldoonians were dying excruciating deaths after rabidly attacking anyone or anything getting in their way. Slogar knew now that the Q'Arons still used biological warfare, a most despicable practice that had been outlawed in the two empires' peace treaty hundreds of years ago. The virus was supposedly destroyed along with all references for its production. Now to find what the Empire had done to eradicate the virus. Where was the passage on treatment and prevention? 'Ah. Here it is,' he stopped his search abruptly. 'Let me see. The virus cannot survive in extreme temperatures, hot or cold. That explains the tales Grandfather used to tell us stories of people who had lost their fingers and toes during the Great Epidemic of Boldoon. I thought he was just senile; what sort of disease would take that extreme a temperature to eradicate it? Why didn't they look for a better way? Surely they knew of the post-exposure prophylaxis treatment. If only we could find some infected victims, animal or human. If only…'

"Dr. Slogar, are you in there?" The guard had broken through Slogar's intense study by banging on the door loud enough to wake the dead. "Dr. Slogar, open the door. We've come to escort you to Clandil." Slogar hoisted himself up after securing his computer back in his equipment bag.

"Give an old man a moment, will you? I'm moving as fast as I can." He slid away the heavy bar to let the guards in. He noted that Cam had sent four guards, not the two he was expecting. The increased number punctuated how vital his part in this mission really was - and the level of danger. He led the men into the kitchen. "Here, Gentlemen. I'll brew you some tea before we set out. Who knows when we'll get such nice accommodations again?" The guards made sure the house was secure; then they returned to the kitchen to find Dr. Slogar whistling along with the tea kettle.

Mara and Grunden
Leave the Cottage

Mara looked back only briefly at the home she and Ram had shared with the precious daughter. It was as if she were in some incredibly sick nightmare from which she could not awaken. The sand impaling itself in her skin reminded her to pull her protective face shield down. Grunden was already several strides ahead of her. With nightfall so near, she shook herself out of her reverie and raced against the sand and wind to catch him. For more than an hour they trudged through the shifting terrain, pushing ever harder so that they could reach what appeared to be a cave on the horizon.

Grunden halted pulling Mara close so she could hear his shout. "We don't have much time left. Do you think you can make it?" Mara knew that she had not been traveling as fast as Grunden would have liked, but she was much smaller and had great difficulty with the pack she bore. Despite her intense desire to collapse on the spot, if only for a moment, she thrust herself forward without answering. Grunden, sensing her dilemma, reached out and pulled the pack from her shoulders. Mara's smile was lost as Grunden picked up his pace, with head low against the wind and continued his beeline for shelter.

The cave was small, but somewhat sheltered from the wind. "Here, Mr. Grunden. Let me help you unpack. I believe that there are utensils and provisions to make a proper, if meager, meal and some hot tea. You have been so kind, and I have, well, I haven't been very easy to get on with today." Mara busied herself setting up her micro-stove and selecting two home-cooked meals for their supper. The thistle was left to steep on the back of the stove.

"I'm sorry I was so short with you, Mara. I know that you are not used to this kind of travel, but there is something about this place that makes me very uneasy especially when I'm out in the open. It's as if someone or something is watching, waiting." Mara gasped at his words. She had not thought of their danger, only finding Ramar.

"Mr. Grunden, I've been so thoughtless. I will try to do better tomorrow. I just dread the thought of going back out into that hateful wind."

"Well, let's not worry about that now. And if we're going to be traveling together, we've got to stop apologizing for everything. And Mara, please stop calling me Mr. Grunden. My name is Jacar, but my friends call me Jack. I'm starved. Is the food ready yet?" Mara pulled their meals from the stove, carefully opening them. The aroma was mouthwatering. They ate without speaking.

After a bit, Jack sat back from their makeshift table, an abandoned miner's crate, and sighed loudly. "Now that's what I call a meal. Where did you learn to cook like that?"

Mara smiled shyly, "Ram taught me how to cook. When we married I couldn't boil water. And even after he was satisfied that I would not starve should he die before I did . . .," her voice trailed off into a soft whisper. The pain of thinking Ram might be dead was unbearable.

"Mara, I'm sorry. I didn't mean to bring up memories that upset you." Jack reached out to touch her arm, but thought better of it. She lay down near the portable heating unit that Jack had set up while she had cooked supper and buried her face in her arms. A loud rattle outside the cave broke the silence. Jack swiftly rose and went to the mouth of the cave to investigate. The camouflage he and Mara had placed by the entrance had blown over, allowing the now strong gusts of bitter wind to swirl through the cave adding to the chill that was already clinging like icicles to their bones. He stepped outside the cave to replace the covering. Though an annoyance, he welcomed the escape. He didn't know how to comfort this grieving woman, or for that matter, even if he should try. He had never been very comfortable with women, and this was just about the prettiest he'd ever seen. 'Jack, old buddy, put those thoughts out of your mind. The woman is here looking for her husband.' He stepped into the wind, instantly chilled by the icy nighttime temperature. As he reached for a piece of tredon bone to brace his entrance cover, a quicksilver movement near a pile of sandstone not twenty yards away caught his eye. His warrior instinct told him that he had to get Mara out of there fast. Doing that without being seen would be impossible. He drew his weapon, slipped silently back into the cave only to find it empty.

On close examination of the rear of the cave, Jack found a dark nook that he had not seen before. By holding his lamp high above his head and peering over the pile of boulders that were stacked around it, he could see that it was the entrance to a tunnel. Without looking back, he stepped over the obstacle and squeezed his broad shoulders through the opening. Jack had gone perhaps a quarter of a mile when he heard a noise up ahead. He quickly doused the light and quietly inched forward in the pitch dark, moving toward the soft blue glow coming from somewhere in front of him. As he started to step into the center of the tunnel from his position along the wall, a rasping voice warned him back. Looking into the darkness he saw nothing but could feel a presence within striking distance. Hand to weapon, Jack turned, ready to defend himself.

"Stow your weapon, mate. You'll get no fight from me. I've come to help you, Jack Grunden." Grunden wondered how this man, if he was a man, could see him in the dark tunnel and how he knew his name. Things were getting stranger by the second – and as those seconds passed he was painfully aware that Mara might be slipping farther and farther away. There was no time to question the stranger; he had to press on. Turning on his heel, he swiftly strode once more into the center of the tunnel where the ceiling was high enough to allow him to stand unimpeded and walk with more ease. Risking attack from the rear, he raced ahead coming so rapidly upon an open chamber bathed in the blue light that he had to take a quick step back into the dark tunnel and surreptitiously study what he saw. He noticed with relief that the air in the chamber was cool and gently moving, like a caress, over his tired sweaty body.

The chamber itself was perhaps one hundred feet across, roughly round in shape with five tunnel openings around the perimeter. In the center was an elevated pedestal from which he could see a delicate hand and slender arm limply lying over the side. He recognized the thin gold band on that hand. It was Mara, lying there so still, too still. As he was about to enter the chamber, Jack heard a cry so bloodcurdling he feared this was the gate to hell with one of its demons preparing to claim a sacrificial offering. As he crouched in the tunnel, he knew once again, he was not alone. A rough hand grabbed him and pulled him so close he could smell the tredon leather of the man's clothes. Jack hoped this was one of the Creedorian rebels who had been outlawed by Jarlod, but whom most everyone else viewed as heroes for trying to remain free and keep Creedor's own culture alive and safe from the Empire censors. Banishment had forced the rebels to live a harsh existence which included depending on stray tredons for food and clothing. If not a rebel, then his other guess would be an escaped slave; which was better — or worse — he didn't have a clue. Grunden knew he was in danger, but was at this moment unsure from what.

The Empire Museum in Clandil

If Slogar had known that Clandil was so far from the cozy cottage, he would have stayed. But here he was now, and armed with his new knowledge, he was ready to begin actual scientific experiments with samples from some of the epidemic victims who had not yet reached the final stages of the illness.

The lab at Clandil had been preserved in pristine condition as part of the Empire Museum. Commander Camdus had made sure it was closed and secured for Dr. Slogar's use. The lab was fine for many of his experiments, but he could see that he would need some of the more advanced implements found only on Andalla. He called his young assistant to him. "Waldo, please contact Commander Camdus. Tell him I need to speak to him at once." Waldo acknowledged with a salute and swiftly left for the communication center. Commander Camdus was still on the mother ship waiting for word from the landing party.

When the call came, Camdus was in his quarters trying to catch a few winks. He snatched the communicator from his bedside table. "Commander, Waldo here. Dr. Slogar wishes to speak to you." Cam waited to hear Slogar's voice, before shouting, "Where the hell are you and why haven't you called in before now? We were afraid something had happened to you and your escort." He could hear Slogar wheezing as he responded. "Cam, we're here on Creedor, where you sent us, at the Clandil Museum lab. There are quite a few things I need before I can get anything significant done. Can you get them for me?" Camdus swore. "You haven't answered my question. And where is Mr. Grunden? He hasn't called in either." At that, Slogar's voice became low and urgent. "Cam, Grunden and the woman were supposed to have been in contact with you hours ago. I thought that you'd have heard from them by now. Arrrgh, I need a drink – bad."

Camdus knew that Slo couldn't take stress without giving in to his craving, but he couldn't let him lose it now. He mentally summoned his assistant. Ensign Rax, the only known subspace particle rider, popped into the room, coming to a disheveled halt before his commander. Cam looked at Rax. Message received. With a nod, Rax was instantly gone.

"Listen, Slo. I know how tough this is for you. I get it, okay? Don't do anything foolish; I'll see to it that you get two transcaps right away. That should get you through this rough spot. You know that I've got to keep you sober. And now you have to tell me all you know about Grunden and the woman. Where were they heading and when was Grunden supposed to rejoin you?" Slogar took the transcaps from Rax, who had just "popped" into the room.

"Damn, Camdus. You could've given me a heart attack. Next time, give me some warning before you send the Rider, how 'bout it?" He needed the transcaps so badly that he didn't even ask how Cam had ordered them while they were still talking. All he could think about was calming this damned craving. After the brief wait it always took for the pills to work, Slogar tried to answer Cam's questions.

"You know as much as I do. Mara Tonlin was determined to find her husband who she said had been abducted by intruders, whoever they are. The story she told was pretty unbelievable, but Grunden had already checked the outbuildings. He was convinced she was telling the truth and that whoever or whatever we're dealing with here is not to be taken lightly. He thinks that in finding her husband, he will also find out exactly what's going on down here. I'm afraid that his initial request for permission to travel with the woman may have been rash, for now it looks as if we should have sent some of your finest with them, just in case. About when he was to rejoin me, that was left open. I thought he had cleared that with you."

Camdus grimly took this in. Now he had no choice but to follow up with another armed unit. He could only hope it was not too late. He had not planned for a secondary mission that would create more problems than he already had. But since Grunden was a Reglon Empire Guard soldier, Cam was duty bound to try to find him, with or without the fool-hearted woman. After checking in with Command, he decided he should lead the unit, leaving Captain Slag with the ship. Cam did not like the way this was shaping up, but without an alternative he began to prepare himself for his journey. Alone in his quarters, he said a silent prayer that God would watch over him and his men. They had the strength and courage, but they could surely use the Almighty's help. Holstering his custom-made weapon, he picked up his helmet and strode to the pod launch to brief his hand-selected unit. As he scanned their seasoned faces, he saw that they were wary but not afraid; this was the mark of skilled warriors. These were men he could trust with his life and had more times than he cared to remember over the years they had spent together in the Emperor's service. Briefing over, the small band boarded their pods with Commander Camdus in the lead looking gravely over the brown planet on which they soon would test their mettle once again. According to the map, the trizactl mines were northwest of the plateau where Dr. Slogar and Mr. Grunden had come upon the woman.

By air it was not a bad trip even with the wind, but over land it must have been rough. Cam wondered if Grunden and the woman had gotten there without falling victim to the ravenous sands – or worse. He landed on a hidden lea not far from what according to the map was a lesser tunnel. Easing the lead pod down, Cam marked the landing of the others until they were safely down. Quickly they engaged the automatic camouflage feature on each landing pod and silently prepared to enter the mines.

Ram explores his surroundings

Li'Let seldom slept, Ram observed. He often awoke to find her staring at him. He wondered how she could survive seemingly with so little sleep. He had never seen her eat, either. As for him, he was too tired to eat most of the time and felt so wrung out that he wasn't sure how much longer he would survive. It was all he could do to dress each day. At least she was letting him wear his own clothes again, though he wondered why they had taken them in the first place. Li'Let smiled as he looked up at her. As she often did, she had been watching him as he slept. Perhaps that explained some of the bizarre nightmares he'd been having lately. Occasionally, when he was sure she was nowhere around, he plotted ways to escape her. His wariness had rapidly turned to hatred. No one should ever have to endure the humiliation he had to face each day. He had figured out pretty quickly that he literally was nothing more than her plaything and often he thought that perhaps she was the cat and he was the mouse. And he knew that, just like a cat when it tires of its prey, Li'Let would dispose of him when he no longer amused her. He caught himself before he let these thoughts creep to the forefront of his mind, especially right at this moment.

He saw her sleek, well-groomed eyebrow arch as if a question mark. "Oh, what's the matter with my boy? Don't you like Li'Let anymore? If you prefer, I could send you to the mines or, better yet I could let Lars play with you awhile. He is a bit heavy handed, but you're a big guy; you wouldn't get hurt – well not too badly anyway." She broke off with a bizarrely high-pitched cackle that sent a chill down his spine. He began saying the "Mary had a little lamb" nursery rhyme over and over in his head.

"Oh. Well, I see how it is; I heard Daddy say there's a new supply for me to play with anyway. I think I'll send you to Lars."

Leveling his eyes to hers, he said, "Let's play." The maze appeared. She forgot about Lars – at least for the moment.

After the game, Li'Let went back to her private chamber. Ramar assessed his situation. He knew his time was running short and now was the opening he had been waiting for to learn more about his environment, and if possible, to devise an escape plan. He had learned early on that the only time Li'Let couldn't read his thoughts, if she so chose, was when she was sleeping or not near him. In the beginning, she never left him. There was no respite from her constant gaze. But lately, she left him for several hours at a time each day. He had no idea what she did after she left him, but he used this time to continue exploring his prison.

Ram first checked to see who was guarding him today. He was surprised to see no one outside his chamber. Carefully opening the chamber door, Ram stepped into the dark hall. An eerie quiet permeated the air. Once he got his bearings, he decided to head back to the holding cells to see if he could find Stadar. Hugging the wall he silently and swiftly covered the distance from his chamber to the cells. No sounds came from within.

"Stad," he whispered. Nothing. "Stad, are you in there?" He realized that the key to the cell was hanging above the door. What was this?! Some sort of trap to ensure his demise? He'd have to risk it. He quietly took the key and opened the cell door, holding his breath as he did so. He slipped inside, closing the door behind him. He pocketed the key and moved deeper into the cell, which seemed to be empty. As his eyes adjusted to the almost pitch dark, he saw a lump in the corner. He carefully poked the mass. A barely audible moan caught his ear as he leaned closer. "Stad," he whispered again.

"Ram, you've got to get out of here; they may be back soon." Ram reached down and lifted the slight figure of his old friend. He carried him to the opening at the back, stepping over the broken barrier. He didn't give Stad a chance to argue; he just took him. He'd lost too much already; if he could save Stad, then by God, he would. Once out of the enclave, he raced for cover against the howling wind. He saw that there was a clump of rugged miracle bushes that seemed to be about the only shrub that could endure this climate. He knew that getting to the center of the clump would be painful as the bushes were full of hateful little thorns. Pushing their way through, they finally found safety within. One of the secrets of the miracle bushes was they provided absolute protection to anyone who got in. Ram had noticed stray bones on the way in the way – maybe animal, maybe human. Another of the miracle bushes' secrets was that all wounds were healed and all needs met. For as long as they needed this refuge, it would protect them; it had after all, allowed them through with only a few scratches. The miracle of the bushes began to work on Stadar. Ram could see him losing his haggard look and returning to his former vigor. He whispered a fervent '*thank you.*' Ram knew he had to get back to find out all they could about what was going on and to see where everyone had gone. Something major must have happened. He had to find out what.

"Stad, stay here; I'll be back in about an hour," Ramar whispered urgently.

Stad had by this time recovered his strength.

"The hell you say. I'm coming with you. You're gonna need me. How did you get out from under that witch's thumb anyway?" Ram briefly filled him in on the changes he'd observed lately. Stad knew that Ram was right to suspect something big was in the works, but the only way they could find out what was to go back in. One part of him wanted to stay within the miracle bush, but Ram nudged him out of their safe haven back into the wind. They made a bee line back to the mouth of the tunnel and slipped inside as quietly as they had left. Stadar, now rejuvenated, returned to the pile of rags in the corner of the cell to wait until it was time to fight or run. Ram gave him the cell door key and went back to his chamber as softly as he could. He slipped into the room, allowing his eyes to adjust to the soft glow again. Just as he slipped back into the chamber and headed for his cot, he heard someone in the inner chamber, Li'Let's lair as he was prone to think of it. He was busy reciting the nursery rhyme when he realized it that it was not Li'Let but Lt.T'Aron who approached. Though surprised, he was at the same time relieved.

T'Aron barked, "Where have you been, Slave?" Ram thought that he made a mistake coming back in, but he and Stad knew they had to find out everything they could about the Q'Arons and what they were up to. Ram gaugedT'Aron's demeanor and decided that if he had wanted to neutralize him he would have already done it. So he stepped out on faith.

"I just wanted to stretch my legs, so I walked to the perimeter and back." T'Aron didn't speak, studying Ramar intently.

"Where is Mistress Li'Let? What have you done with her?" Ram had not anticipated this development.

"What do you mean, what have I done with her? She left me hours ago, like she does every day. You said it yourself; I'm a slave. I have no weapon; my strength has been sapped; not to mention, I like life too much to risk her wrath."

He perceived a slight easing of T'Aron's stance. "You know, she uses us slaves as a substitute for you, don't you? This vicious game she plays with us is just her venting frustration because she is not allowed to be with you. I mean, you have to have seen how she looks at you. You would be a much better player in the maze than any of us captives. You know her, how she thinks, how she moves. Besides, I'm not sure, but I think if she were allowed to be with you, the maze might just disappear for good."

"Shut up. You have no right to speak of such things. I will recommend the mines for you because of your insolent tongue." Ram knew that his only hope was to try to convince Lt. T'Aron that he could help get Li'Let to follow her desire, if not the law. After all, she didn't seem terribly concerned about anything other than satisfying her own cruel whims.

"Look, I know you care for her. So why don't you let me help? I mean, it may seem twisted, but I am in a position to plant some ideas for you, if you know what I mean."

"Go on," T'Aron ordered.

"Well, she reads my mind far too well, but I can use my thoughts to make her want to play with you, with only you.

Not just as a prey, but as a partner. What do you say? I'll help you with her; you help me to freedom."

T'Aron considered this foolish man, but said nothing. Before either could say anything else, Li'Let entered the chamber. She considered both of these men; one a slave, one a soldier. When T'Aron was in the room, she could no longer think of another man. 'What is this, this strangeness in my chest?' Li'Let saw T'Aron's muscles ripple beneath his shirt as he moved to make room for her. For the slightest moment, they locked gazes. The tension between them was palpable. Ram suddenly felt like an interloper into a very private moment. He quickly moved to the door once again bracing for a nucleo jolt. When none came he slipped out breathing another quick prayer of thanks. Knowing her twisted habits as he did, he felt confident that he had several hours to work on finding the secret to the Hold. As he exited, he could hear their voices, low and tentative, coming from the chamber he had just left. This time, he felt Li'Let would finally face the feelings she had for T'Aron and maybe, just maybe, she would listen to her heart instead of her animal instinct.

Mara's Rescue

Ramar headed back to the cell; the door was closed but unlocked. He entered the cell quietly. The others were still absent; most likely they had been taken to the mine. He swiftly strode to the corner where Stadar lay so completely immobile that Ramar thought him asleep. He knelt beside Stad, touching him on the shoulder. Stadar bolted up off the floor nearly knocking Ram down.

"Hey, it's me. We've got to get out of here – now."

Stadar looked hard into the dark, recognizing Ram's voice. "What are you doing here again so soon? What's happened?"

Ram grabbed his arm and propelled him down the hall-way. "Not now. Let's go." They raced toward the tunnels, disappearing into the nearest one. Once inside they stopped to catch their breath and get their bearings. "Things have changed, Stad. T'Aron is with Li'Let, but I don't know for how long. She has left me for longer and longer in the maze without seriously coming after me. But here's the weird part - she changes in the maze; she becomes some kind of animal, part hound, part lion. I don't know, but I know this: I'm not going back." Stad knew about the maze, but he hadn't played the game so he was sent to Lars for torture.

All Stad could think of was getting out of this hell hole and trying to help free the other Creedorian slaves from the trizactl mines. "Okay, where do we go from here, Ramar?"

Ram had wondered that himself. "Let's see where this tunnel goes." Quietly they edged forward hugging the tunnel wall. The air became warmer as they went. A blue glow filled the mouth of the tunnel where it entered a larger chamber. They heard a noise at the beginning of the tunnel that caused them to stop, stock still. Without a word, they knew they had no time left. The guards must have missed them and were within striking distance. They felt the wall for openings, but only found small crannies too small to stand in, but they were able to hide themselves by crouching within a couple of them. Stadar, whose eyes quickly adapted to the dark, saw the Reglon Empire Guard emblem on the uniform of the man who was now within five feet of them. He recognized Jacar Grunden; he'd served with him some years ago. He grabbed Jack and pulled him back into the tunnel. They froze when they heard a feral cry coming from one of the tunnels on the far side of the chamber ahead. By this time, Ram was standing beside Stad. He too had seen the emblem. Before either of them could make a move, they saw what was making the noise. A huge, ebony beast entered the chamber, and began circling the base of the pedestal. Jack had never seen such an animal. Its eyes glowed deep gold; its razor like teeth jutted so far out that its lip was curled into a permanent snarl. The beast had a shaggy mane like a lion but cloven rear feet like a goat. It took one step up onto the pedestal and poised as if to spring, a low growl rumbling in its chest. They held their breath. At that moment, they heard what sounded like a long low whistle. The animal stopped and listened. The whistle again sounded, and the great beast sprang back and bounded off down the far tunnel.

Carefully, the three men, led by Grunden, entered the chamber. He didn't know how much time they had, but he knew they had to free Mara. Ram had seen that slender hand and known without a doubt that it was his wife who would be sacrificed to the beast if he didn't act fast. Without speaking, Grunden handed each man mini-nucleos. They carefully, but very swiftly, covered the distance across the floor to the pedestal. Ram raced up the steps and leaped to the top. Mara was not bound, but seemed to be barely breathing. He scooped her up and with another great leap landed at the base of the pedestal. As he was racing back to the tunnel, the beast reappeared. Grunden and Stad both took aim and fired. The beast was stunned, but did not go down. With an incredulous glance at each other, they took off behind Ram and Mara. Once far enough into the tunnel to be safe, Grunden blasted the rock above the entrance, causing it to collapse. They saw the furious beast's massive paw, claws extended, pawing at the top of the rubble heap. "Run!" Grunden ordered as they realized the beast was breaching the barricade.

Once outside the tunnel, they found the exit to the yard beyond. Ramar and Stad both knew the miracle bush was their only hope. For once they were glad the demon winds were so fierce because the dust cloud provided them the cover they needed to get to safety. Ram and Stad had an easier time than Grunden, though Mara was allowed to enter unscathed.

Grunden was scraped and scratched, but otherwise, he too was unharmed. "Where are we?" He asked no one in particular.

"You wouldn't believe me if I told you. Tell us who you are and what you're doing here. With my wife," Ram said.

"Easy, Ramar," Stad said firmly. "This is Jacar Grunden. Jack's all right. We served together a few years ago."

Then Stad asked Jack, "What are you doing here? This isn't your normal posting, now is it?"

Grunden said, "Stadar, am I glad that was you in the tunnel! You have no idea what's on the outside. As for me, well, I'm in service to Emperor Jarlod, assigned to Commander Michael Camdus. We came here on a research mission to find a cure for the epidemic on Creedor. But when we got here, we realized that we were faced with the problem of the intruders. To make things worse, we don't know what's causing the epidemic, or who the intruders really are. We took shelter in what we thought was an abandoned house only to find this lady, your wife, who filled us in on what was happening down here."

Jack paused before going on, "So you must be Ramar Tonlin. You have a very brave wife, Mr. Tonlin. Very stubborn, but very brave." Ram was cradling Mara in his arms as Grunden talked. He prayed that she too would heal while they were in the miracle bush. But Mara showed no signs of rousing. Her breathing was very slow and she was so pale. He felt for a pulse, just to reassure himself that she was still with him. She had one, faint though it was. He breathed yet another prayer. Ram leaned down and tenderly kissed her forehead.

Her eyelashes fluttered; then she opened her eyes. "You missed," she said to Ram. He kissed her again, this time gently on the lips. "That's better. I thought I'd never see you again, my husband. God is so good." She snuggled into his shoulder and fell once again into a deep sleep. He placed her on one of the beds of leaves he and Stadar had made when they were here before.

Then he turned to Grunden. "Now what? We can't stay here forever, though I think the miracle bush has granted us haven here and will protect us for as long as we require it."

Stadar had been sitting quietly listening to this exchange. Now he spoke, "There are several ways to enter
the enclave. It'd probably be safe to assume that there are
armed guards at each one. We need a way to get in without being noticed. The way things are now, that would be
pretty hard to do, especially for you, Mr. Grunden. And
then there's the problem of Mara. We can't just leave her
here without anyone to help her. God only knows what
she's endured." At this Ram clenched his teeth. He knew
she was weak right now, but they had to help Grunden
and Stad. They needed another miracle, this time a really
big one.

Grunden checked his communicator and found that it
was working again. He called the Commander. After a brief
chewing out, Grunden explained what had happened, where
they were, and what they needed.

The Commander scoffed, "You're where? What the hell
is a miracle bush? Never mind, just give me the coordinates.
We'll get you out of there."

It took Cam and his men about a half hour to regain his
pod. While they quickly prepared for launch, Cam locked
in on the coordinates Grunden had given him. In a matter
of moments, the pod landed beside the miracle bush, which
looked to Camdus like a huge tangle of weeds. Hearing
the pod land, Grunden followed by Stadar and Ram carrying Mara made their way from their hiding place. Without
a word, they all boarded and buckled in. Grunden and his
companions collectively breathed the relief they all felt as the
pod took off, straight up. Then it zipped across the heavens
to the mother cruiser. Once on board, Mara was taken to the

ship's infirmary while the three men were debriefed in the Commander's quarters.

Camdus looked from his crewman to the two strangers. "All right, Mr. Grunden, who are your companions?"

Grunden spoke, "This man is Ramar Tonlin, the woman Mara's husband. It was their home Dr. Slogar and I used for shelter when we landed on Creedor." He then introduced Stadar. He briefly told the Commander what had happened at the cottage and how he had decided to ask permission to accompany Ramar's wife to find him. He relayed some of the loss the couple had endured, wrapping up with, "The rest of their neighbors and friends were taken into slavery by I don't know who."

Here Ram interrupted, "I know. It's the Q'Arons. They have constructed a huge underground complex they call Q'Door Hold. I was the captive of Li'Let who is the daughter of Thurl, the Master Slaver. You need to know that these beings are not human. They look, sound, and act human, but please believe me when I say they are NOT human. The woman, or beast, Li'Let has a maze behind her chamber where she sets slaves loose, only to come after them. She never caught me because I found a small concealed cavern within one of the walls. She, or it, would come sniffing and growling through the maze to find me. I always fell asleep in the cavern and inevitably found myself back in my prison the following day. I can only surmise that each time the maze disappeared, I was exposed. There was very little rest for any of us. If we didn't prove to be enough sport for her, she would let her sadistic eunuch torture us. I never faced that, but Stadar did."

Stad took over the telling of this incredible story, "Lars was huge; he seemed to resent any man who was still a man and took every opportunity to show me that he was my master. He whipped me with barbs until I nearly bled to death and he fell away exhausted. When I passed out, I was patched up and returned to my cell with the others. If Ramar had not found me and taken me to the miracle bush for healing, I have no doubt I would be dead now."

Camdus remained silent for some time, taking all this in. He needed time to think and to make contact with Dr. Slogar and his dad. Maybe now he could get some of the puzzle pieces to fit. The Q'Arons were ruthless and possessed weapons that the Empire didn't. And who or what were the beasts? What powers did they possess? How could they be defeated?

He turned to Ramar and Stad, "You two need to get some sleep; we have some serious work to do tomorrow." Stad was grateful for the opportunity to clean up, eat, and sleep and told Camdus so. Cam summoned Rax who escorted Stad to his quarters.

Ram asked, "Commander, do you think I could see my wife before I go to my quarters?" Camdus felt a twinge of envy for this man who had a second chance with the love of his life.

"Rax will be back in a few moments," Cam said, "he'll make sure that you are escorted to Mrs. Tonlin. But first, tell me what kind of weapons they have, if you know."

Ram thought a moment and responded, "They all carry side arms similar to ours. I was fortunate to have been spared its sting, so can't say what exactly it does. Then there's the perimeter of the Hold. It's heavily guarded and has the biggest cannons I've ever seen. But I think the change-lings may be their most despicable weapon. I don't know if they can shift into shapes other than the beasts. And I don't know which one is their normal state; either way, we have to watch out for them. Based on the increased activity and their altered behavior for the past two weeks, I'd say they are plan-ning to take a shipment of trizactl back to Q'Aron within the next day or so. Even the guards have been absent most of the time. It's like they almost forgot that Stad and I were still there, or that we didn't matter anymore. Commander, I think they're finished with the planet, but somehow I think they haven't begun to mess with the Empire yet."

When Rax returned, Camdus instructed him to return both men to his quarters at 8:00 sharp the following morn-ing. Rax led Ramar down the quiet corridor to the infirma-ry. They stopped at the third compartment; inside Mara lay sleeping, attached to the diagnostic computer. Rax touched the identity pad, and ushered Ramar in. He handed him a guest card with which to come and go into this compart-ment only. Ram thanked Rax and waited until he was alone with Mara. The soft light fell on her pale face and hair. Ram stood quietly beside the bed, watching his beautiful Mara. She looked so peaceful, but he knew from his own experi-ence that she had to have suffered great fear. He sat down in the chair beside her bed and gently took her hand. Her sleep was so deep that she didn't respond to his touch. But she was alive, and he knew that with life there is hope. He leaned over, laying his head beside her. He prayed with his whole heart, drifting to sleep while still in prayer. He awoke sometime later to find Mara stroking his hair. When he sat up, he saw his Mara smiling at him. He knew that his prayers had been answered. He and Mara were talking an hour later, when the infirmary attendant came in to check on Mara.

"Ah, so you must be Mr. Tonlin. Let me ease your mind; she's going to be fine. Look at this read out. The CompuDoc indicates that she is merely exhausted. She will be released first thing tomorrow if all her vitals are at normal levels. But tonight she and you from the looks of things need sleep." Ram thanked the attendant, kissed his wife, and stepped into the corridor.

Rax appeared as if from nowhere beside him. Had he not been so exhausted he might have been startled. "Follow me, Mr. Tonlin." Ramar followed Rax to his quarters. He was pleased to see that there would be ample room for Mara.

He thanked Rax, who offered to bring him supper. "No thank you, Rax. I just want to shower and sleep. Goodnight."

The next morning, Ram had already been to check on Mara, who was excited about her imminent release. He listened to his excited wife. She could hardly wait to have time with her husband again, but felt a pang of sadness when she realized that they may never be able to go home again. "But really," she wondered aloud, "what is there anymore? Nothing but a cottage and painful memories." She was bracing herself for what was to come. She told Ram that she was looking at it as a grand journey that they were embarking on together. Now she smiled that beautiful smile that always made him smile, too. Listening to her chatter comforted him, but he knew there were many other things that they needed to know. When Rax appeared with Stadar, Ram gave Mara a gentle hug, kissed her brow, and left her with a whispered something that made her blush. They were taken to the dining hall where they ate their fill of simple food that was good and hot. After eating this much needed breakfast, Ram and Stadar were escorted by Rax to their meeting with Commander Camdus.

"Good morning, Gentlemen. Please come in and have a seat." Camdus showed them to the sofa opposite him. "I've spoken to some of my sources and have learned a little, but I need to know more details. We've got to be missing something. Stadar, please go back to the beginning. How exactly did they capture you?" Stadar had to think a minute. It seemed like a lifetime ago he had been getting ready to do some consulting work at the office of the Reglon mines. He had stepped outside his house just like always. That's the last thing he remembered until he woke up in the cell in Q'Door Hold.

"Commander, I have no idea how they did it. One minute I was outside my house getting ready to enter my pod; the next I was spread-eagled on the floor of what I now know is Q'Door Hold. I didn't see, hear, or feel anything."

Camdus knew that there had to be something, no matter how small, that might give them a clue. So he pressed Stadar, "Think. Go back to that morning. Describe everything around you. Take your time. This is important."

Stadar looked at Camdus in disbelief. Had he not just told him he didn't remember? Oh well. He'd try. "When I first stepped out of the house, the pod was where it always is, hovering just to the right of the door; I have a special permit to use a pod as the work I've been doing is high priority for my company. It's a zero emissions pod, mind you. I guess you already know that the company I work for is responsible for maintaining private security equipment to some of the world's most affluent citizens as well as many military installations. With my security clearance, I've been able to access locations that are off limits to many of my superiors." Camdus listened impatiently but tried not to let it show. Stadar read the impatience anyway, and clearing his throat, continued. "As I said, everything was the same. There was a light breeze. Traffic on the moving sidewalk had halted, as it sometimes does when too many people are trying to ride. People were standing around, some grousing about being late, others chatting together...." He stopped. How could he have missed it!? "I can't believe I didn't pay it any attention. One of the people on the sidewalk stepped over the side. He actually got off. I was so busy thinking about the work I had to tackle I noticed it but wasn't alarmed. But now, in looking back, that was definitely not normal. No one EVER gets off the sidewalk, not even if it stalls for an hour or more. But this person did."

Camdus was sitting on the edge of his seat, "Stadar, what did the man look like? How was he dressed? I want to know every single detail."

Stad didn't have to think too hard, "He was very tall and somewhat thin. I remember that his uni was as black as night. I'm sorry, but I never saw his face. I don't remember anything else after he bounded over the rail."

Camdus asked one more question, "Did he have long, black hair?"

Stad closed his eyes, trying to remember. "As a matter of fact, he did. Why?"

Camdus inhaled sharply. "If he is who I think he is, our troubles are just about to get a whole lot worse. Serin of Killund is a much sought after mercenary, offering a menu of services that include the most heinous of crimes. It's clear to me that he is the one who kidnapped you. I am guessing he also took your pod, which is how he transported you and has increased his mobility significantly. Now we know he has signed on with the Q'Arons, and he has shown that he is as ruthless as always." Stad took this in stoically.

Camdus turned to Ram, "I need to hear the details of your capture and your imprisonment, since you seem to have spent the most time in the direct company of the enemy."

Ram had been listening intently. Now it was his turn to speak. "I was soaking my chilled bones in a hot bath trying to get warm as much as to get the grit out of every crevice of my body. Just as I was drifting off to sleep in the still warm water, Mara yelled for me to come to the front room. I grabbed my clothes, dressing as I went. She was babbling about being rescued. We secured the house and Mara went to the safe room. When I was certain Mara was safe, I took my weapon, slipped out of the house and raced to the barn. From my hiding place in one of the empty stalls, I heard them before I saw them. The sound of someone kicking in the cottage door made me furious, but I held my position. I knew Mara was hidden and hoped she stayed that way. After a few moments, the door to the barn slammed open, banging against the side. The animals went berserk. The intruders, hooded and armed with lethal weapons, slaughtered the tredons, ripping them apart and feeding on them. The last animal down was Abalon. The mare wheeled and reared, her hooves slashing her attacker, sending his yellow blood flying.

It only made the attacker more vicious. Eyes flared wide with fear, the horse went down. Her attacker went down after her, ripping her throat out with his hands. I couldn't take it. I stepped out, took aim and blasted him. It didn't faze him; he went back to his meal. I blasted him again, drawing more of his hateful yellow blood. This time, he rose and sneered at me. The next thing I knew, I was lying on the floor of a cell in Q'Door Hold. There were others there, besides me and Stad. They were shackled, and I soon realized that I was, too. It wasn't long before Li'Let and company came to 'inspect' us."

Cam stopped him to ask a question, "Tell me who was with her. Start with the guards."

"I never caught the name of one of the guards who must have been a lackey, but the other was called T'Aron. He's Li'Let's assistant and personal body guard. He's smart and brave. But he has a weakness: Li'Let. They are really attracted to each other but apparently Q'Aron law forbids their union. Just before we escaped, they were finally having a conversation of equals, not mistress and servant. The last member of the party was an old man who bore the torch. They called him Slafe. The only thing that stood out about him was the ring he wore."

Camdus interrupted, urgency in his voice, "Tell me about the ring, Ram. What was unusual about it?"

"The ring was big," Ram continued, "with a large diamond in the center. It was flanked by rubies and the letter 'V' sitting in golden entwined serpents. I didn't have time at that moment to consider how odd it was that this old servant possessed such a valuable piece. But now, knowing what I do about the Q'Arons, it doesn't make sense."

There was no doubt in Cam's mind as to who this was, and his name was not Slafe; it was Elsnor. He was a contemporary of the banished wizard Vandalen. How had he gotten into the Q'Arons' midst? A more pertinent question might be, 'Whose side was he really on?'

Willem and Tomer:
Back in the Saddle

Willem and Tomer agreed to meet at a small restaurant, The Captain's Table, on the east side of the Jevishal, a rapid river that ran through the heart of Capitol City. Its waters were thought to have curative powers, if drawn on the first night that both moons shown in the southern sky simultaneously, an event that happened once every 500 years. As far as either of them knew, this was nothing more than a myth. The ancient pedestrian bridge that spanned the river was void of traffic when Will crossed it. He stopped midway, at its highest point, to look out over the city. There was something intriguing about watching the people below gliding along on the moving sidewalks. He wondered what would happen if someone wanted to get off and just walk on the ground. But then most folks thought there would be no the point of walking when they could ride. Everything seemed to be so orderly, so peaceful. How much longer that would hold true, he had no idea. When the evening sky turned a dark bluish purple, he continued his trek to the restaurant. Tomer was already there waiting for him. He had secured one of the private booths with heavy curtains that they would close after dinner was served.

"Lenwood, so glad you could join me this evening. Would you like some wine?" Tomer played the sophisticate impeccably.

"Why thank you, Old Boy," Will replied with a twinkle in his eye.

Tomer summoned the waiter, who took their order and disappeared. He returned shortly with a bottle of chardonnay.

The wine was mediocre at best, but neither commented. After their supper of steak and fresh salad was served, the waiter closed the curtain. Willem secured their conversation's privacy by activating the tiny device he wore as a ring. He'd used it decades ago during his service years. It was the kind of thing that during those years was expendable, thus no one was ever asked to account for them. He had been relieved to find that it still worked.

"What have you learned about Enright?" Willem leaned over and poured more wine. The fresh bread was so warm the tredon butter melted into it. He took a bite of steak, slowly chewing as he listened to Tomer.

"You know his position was a political appointment. My former assistant, Dormax, came in one morning and tendered a two week notice. I didn't think much of it, since he said he was leaving to spend more time with his family. Since your visit the other day, I've done some quiet investigating. Dormax's family said he was home for maybe a week before he told them he had to get back to the office for important business. Of course, he never returned. None of my contacts have been able to find him, but they believe that he was given an unregistered pod. There's no telling where he is by now."

Will digested this news, seeing clearly how this tied to Enright. Someone wanted Dormax replaced with their agent to carry out whatever they needed done. He knew from what Michael had told him that Enright had withheld reports from Tomer that would have revealed the intruder's activities. But who had that kind of pull?

Willem finally understood, at least in part, "Well that piece of the puzzle is at least identified, but how does it fit? Better question: Who put it on the board?"

Tomer didn't hesitate to speculate, "Weilz. It had to be the Prime Minister. He's the only one who stands to gain by Jarlod's fall. But knowing that just raises more questions. How long has he been in league with Q'Aron? What else has he done? Was Enright his only henchman? …."

"Hold on, Tomer, we have to focus on one thread at a time. What information did Enright have access to?"

Tomer thought a moment. "He was my assistant, but I didn't know him well so I only gave him access to data concerning troop assignments. He had no knowledge of our newest weaponry; at least I don't think he did."

Willem listened intently, slowly digesting his meal and the new information. "So he knew what areas would be easier to slip through. But what was his reward? We need to know whether he was a traitor or a victim. Tomer, you have to get back to your office and see what you can find out. But be careful; Weilz is capable of anything, if he's the top level traitor. Contact me, Lenwood, as soon as you know. Mrs. Radfield and I would love to have you visit – soon. We'll arrange it as we did this time. Now, how about dessert?"

Will was reaching for the curtain when his communicator alerted him to a call from his son. He dropped his hand, re-activated the privacy ring, and answered, "Michael, what a nice surprise." Will gave Tomer a cautionary look.

"Dad, have you found anything out yet?" Camdus asked his father. Willem filled Cam in on Enright and the Prime Minister.

"Enright. I was in the academy with Matthew Enright. If it's the same one, I dated his sister Rayalla for several months. When his father Major Christoff Enright was promoted, they moved to Killund, where his father was in command of all the planet troops. Matt seemed like an ordinary sort. Are you sure?"

"Quite. But we're not sure if his assistance is voluntary or coerced. Tomer will try to find out when he gets back to his office tomorrow. What's going on at your end?" Cam gave his dad the quick and dirty, making sure to tell him about Elsnor, and then bade him goodnight.

Rayalla. For years, he had forced thoughts of her from his heart. They had fallen into a tender, magical sort of relationship that tiptoed around commitment. Camdus knew that Rayalla and he could have had a life together that would have been one adventure after another. But then life happened and they were forced to set each other free. Many times in the early years after their separation, Cam had wondered if Rayalla had been able to find freedom to love again; he knew that she still held his heart and until he found closure on that chapter of his life, he could never think seriously about another woman. He had to focus on the issue at hand. What of Matt? This just did not mesh with the Matt Enright he knew. He and Matt had been in the same class, shared meals, gotten drunk together. His head began to thump soundly, the pain driving out his ability to problem-solve. He touched on his classical music, adjusted the sound to a softer level and retired for the night. He needed to be on his game from here on in; this journey down memory lane had accomplished nothing. He couldn't afford to take that trip again.

The next day he met with Grunden to apprise him of what he'd learned from his father and what he suspected had happened to Elder Arking's assistant Dormax and, most likely, to Enright's sister as well.

Serin at Q'Door Hold

"The Creedorian was too easy to collect. What sort of world is this that its people live in herds with no independent thought? It's a good thing for them I didn't come here for sport. I have delivered the Creedorian Stadar to you. I will be on my way at first light. I trust you've enhanced my account with the agreed upon sum?" Serin lounged carelessly in a large chair by a stone hearth crackling with blue flame. His long hair was drawn back in a low ponytail.

Elsnor stood staring into the fire. No longer dressed as the old man servant, he wore splendid royal blue robes with a large golden Q suspended from a heavy gold necklace. He stood soldier straight, remaining silent as Serin spoke. "Yes, Serin, we have made the transfer. Unfortunately, we will not be able to let you leave just yet. I'm sure your accommodations are comfortable."

Serin did not care for Elsnor's tone. "I hope you know you cannot keep me here against my will, Elsnor. Many have tried; none have succeeded."

Elsnor looked at Serin, the faintest smile teasing his mouth. "Perhaps. But I was not among them." The seasoned mercenary, occasional assassin, felt a chill run the length of his spine. His survival mode kicked in; he sprang from the chair and lunged at Elsnor only to find himself flung hard into a far wall. Elsnor had not moved from his place at the hearth, but was now facing the stunned assailant. "As I said, Serin, I'm sure you will continue to find your accommodations quite comfortable."

Serin had underestimated the old man. This was a mistake that he prided himself in never making. But how had

Elsnor repelled the attack? Serin was unable to move for several moments. When he rose, Elsnor was still standing by the hearth, but studying his every move. "Why are you holding me? I have performed my contractual duties. What reason could you possibly have for keeping me here — against my will, at that?"

Elsnor studied Serin as if watching a fly struggling to free itself from a web; he then answered, "You are a mercenary. Until our mission is complete, I cannot allow one of your trade to leave, perhaps to work for the enemy. The alternative to your remaining my guest is not one you would prefer, I'm sure."

Serin knew that for the first time in his career he had been outmatched, and by an old man, at that. He rose from the floor, made sure his legs were steady and walked from the room with as much dignity as he could muster.

Back in his quarters, he knew he had to figure a way out of this. He lay back on his bed, arms folded under his head, to think. He had been around long enough to recognize the Trilvarian wizard ring on Elsnor's hand. Everyone remembered the awesome powers that Vandalen had possessed. Serin had been most pleased when Vandalen had been banished to Dartal. Jarlod's men had caught Vandalen in one of the rare moments when he was not wearing his ring. It was rumored that Jarlod had tried to use the ring, but found it to be totally void of any power. In a fit of rage, the rumor went, he flung the ring into the Jevishal River, which curved behind the Emperor's palace and flowed directly beneath his great room window. As for Serin, he figured that the ring actually did have the power, but only Vandalen knew how to access it.

Yet here he was - a prisoner to Elsnor who wore an identical ring. What was the connection, if there was one? And if they were connected, how had it escaped his knowledge? With these thoughts rumbling through his throbbing head, Serin drifted into a troubled sleep.

Next morning, Serin was awakened by the sound of his door opening. He lay still, waiting. He knew his only weapons were his bare hands and his experience, but they had always been more than enough. He listened. Nothing. After a few more minutes, Serin slipped from his bed and silently walked to the seating area. A beautiful woman sat, legs crossed, looking him directly in the eye. "Good morning, Serin. I hope I haven't disturbed your sleep." Serin had seen this woman before; no man could ever forget her porcelain skin and jet black hair. She was dressed in a black uni, much like his own, but far more feminine.

"Who are you and why are you in my room?" The woman rose, strode to him and stopped just short of being too close for comfort. "I am Li'Let. And I have been sent here to keep you occupied for a bit."

Serin didn't like the look in her coal black eyes. He couldn't see, not really see, into them. It was as if she was a shell housing a dangerous inhabitant. "I'm sure I do not need to be occupied, as you put it. I am quite content to while away my imprisonment here alone."

Li'Let clicked her tongue at him. "Imprisonment is such a nasty word. Shall we just call this your extended stay?"

Serin was seriously ticked off now. "Call it what the hell you like. I call it imprisonment. All I want is to make sure

my funds are intact and to be on my way. I have other obliga-
tions I must complete in short order or forfeit my fee, not
that you give a damn."

Li'Let's low growl that tried to masquerade as a laugh
made the hairs on the back of his neck stand up. Serin's
disgust was evident, and Li'Let made it clear to him that
she didn't like it. With one step she was on him, with his
arm twisted brutally behind him. How had he let this happen – again? First the old man, now a woman. His man-
hood threatened, he counter twisted and brought her down
with a knee to her belly. If she wanted to fight like a man,
then by the gods, she would have to take it like a man. She
screamed in agony, sprang back and came at him again, slashing his uni with her long claw-like nails. He felt a sharp pain
where the claws dug deep. His rage exploded with a scream.
He grabbed her arm and slung her backwards into the steel
door, not letting go of her wrist. At that moment, the door
opened to reveal a Q'Aron warrior with his weapon drawn.
With instinct alone, he pulled the woman back and held her
in front of him just in time to take the full blast. She instantly crumpled, lifeless to the floor. The man knelt beside
her; the look on the warrior's face was unmistakable. Serin
knew in that second that his only chance was to grab the nucleo before the man regained his composure. Serin knocked
the weapon out of the man's hand, chased it across the floor
and fled out of the still open door. As he raced down the
long hallway of Q'Door Hold, he heard a blood curdling
scream. If he didn't find a way out soon, he was certain he'd
be keeping his appointment with the Dark Master before his
appointed time. He heard the thudding of feet coming after
him. The door to the slaves' cell lay wide open. He dashed
into the dark space, bruising himself as he ran into jagged

rock that protruded from the walls. He felt a gust of air near the back of the enclosure; he raced to it, still unable to see. Once over the pile of rocks, the demon winds lashed at him nearly as hard as the woman's claws. 'Now what?' he thought as he raced into the blinding storm. He fell into a prickly bush that clawed at him, gouging chunks of flesh from him. He screamed and literally tore himself away, racing into the storm. The winds swirled faster and the sand abraded his badly torn body. Serin stumbled over a jutting rock and fell face first into the sand. Rolling over, the last thing he saw before losing consciousness was the glowing eyes of a huge cat. His screams were lost in the demon winds. Thinking its prey dead, the beast returned to Q'Door Hold, its anger spent.

Back to Q'Door Hold

The time before this dawn was filled with the business of getting ready for what they all sensed would be the most dangerous mission yet. They had been to Q'Door Hold once, only to have to abort to save the woman Mara Tonlin and her party. But this time there'd be no turning back. Whoever or whatever was in Q'Door Hold was their target.

The four pods flew in camo mode this time because they knew the enemy was not the garden variety. They possessed strange powers and incredible weapons. The invisi-shields alone were trouble. Who knew where they had gone, undetected, utterly invisible. And the changelings presented yet another problem. They knew there was at least one of them, Li'Let, who was a formidable foe.

The pods landed this time at the plateau near the mouth of the north tunnel. The wind buffeted them, but their auxiliary stabilizers held. Slipping from the pods into the demon winds in their sand colored uniforms, they seemed to disappear. Camdus took the lead as they struck out for their pre-arranged destination. After about fifteen minutes of fighting headlong through the wind and sand, they gathered to the left and right of the tunnel. Cam motioned Grunden to make sure his party was ready; then they entered. Grunden, Stadar, Ramar, and two more armed soldiers entered quietly behind Camdus, Rax, Slag and their two soldiers. Once inside they realized the passageway was much narrower than they were expecting and would require them to go single file. Grunden sent his party ahead of him, assigning himself the duty of covering their backs. Ten men in a tunnel this small was treacherous at best. Ahead they felt a blast of hot air coming up from somewhere below. Though finding warmth underground was disconcerting, the men welcomed a break from the bitter, cold wind outside. Progress was slow, but steady. Shortly they came upon a side passageway that branched off the main tunnel. Cam decided to take Rax and Slag and explore it, while leaving the two soldiers to guard the entryway. Grunden saw where they were going, and held up to see if the Commander would summon them to follow. Camdus gestured for Grunden to take his men on through the main tunnel. Silently the two parties moved apart, yet ever closer to the center of Q'Door Hold.

Grunden heard a low rumbling coming from somewhere beyond their position. 'Strange,' he thought, 'I don't remember the beast's growl being so low. Must be a different one; that can't be good.' He slowed his column down; he had engaged one of these beasts before and wanted to avoid another encounter, if at all possible. Ram and Stadar, followed by the other soldiers, also heard the animal. This nightmare seemed to have no end.

Grunden edged along the tunnel, stopping just short of the inner chamber which was no more than a widening of the tunnel. The sound of the beast had receded so he felt that it would be safe to enter. Just in case, he motioned to the others to hang back a bit. The chamber was smaller than the one where Mara had been held so he figured that Q'Door Hold must be like an ant hill of sorts with tunnels and secondary chambers leading, he hoped, to the main chamber where he was almost positive the Q'Arons had their headquarters. He made mental notes of the oddly colored layers of stone running through the walls of the chamber; he had learned a long time ago that sometimes the most insignificant details might be useful later. But he was getting worried about the Commander, who hadn't contacted him yet. He tried to raise him but got nothing. He signaled the rest of his party to join him. Stadar and Ram entered, followed by the others.

Grunden spoke softly, "We've lost contact with the Commander. Either they've run into some pretty thick tunnel walls, or they've been taken. We need to find them. You two were here. Maybe you'll remember something that can help." Ram and Stad exchanged a look that was unmistakable. What they remembered they hoped they never had to think of again. But Grunden was right. They had to find the Commander.

After inspecting the small chamber's perimeter, they were pretty sure that only a Rider would be able to access it without using the tunnel. Lucky for them Rax was on their side. Satisfied that the tunnel was what it appeared to be and not a trick, they quietly passed through the center and went into the tunnel on the other side. They pressed onward until they saw another chamber up ahead, this one enormous by comparison to the others. They approached it very carefully, its blue light pulsating eerily ahead like a palpable warning.

From the shadows of the tunnel, Grunden studied the chamber for a moment. The center contained a huge tube of steel and glass. There was a double door at the floor level. This had to be a transport tube. But transport to where, and if they got on, could they get off alive? Making quick decision, he whispered to his team, "I'm going in; if I'm not back in 20 minutes, go back to the Commander's tunnel and find him. He'll know what to do." He waited for the light to pulse off, leaving the chamber black for about three seconds. On black, he strode to the door and touched it. It didn't open. The light pulsed back on, with Grunden plastered to the door. Black again, he gave the door a jolt from his mini nucleo. It opened. He breathed a prayer and stepped on. The door closed; the transport seemed to launch upwards, throwing Grunden to the floor. In an instant, it jerked to a halt and he jumped to his feet, weapon ready. The door opened onto a wide empty foyer. As soon as he stepped off, the tube lurched on its journey to a level somewhere above him. Quickly getting his bearings, Grunden took off down the corridor to his right. He hadn't gone far when he heard loud, angry voices. He chanced a surreptitious look around the corner. A very large officer was looking down at what appeared to be a messenger.

"Breached? Impossible! It has to be a malfunction," one of the Q'Aron officers was saying to the hapless guard who had the unhappy task of reporting the warning to his superior.

He quickly ducked back around the corner. He looked for a place to hide and found nothing but solid wall until a piece of the wall slid open and he fell sideways into a small dark room, no more than a large closet, really. He stood very still, listening while he let his eyes adjust to the darkened room. He was able to make out three others in the room. They appeared to be asleep on their feet. He carefully approached them. The first one he didn't recognize. But the second he knew immediately: Dormax. To the left of Dormax stood a woman he could only assume was Enright's sister Rayalla. That would explain Enright's involvement in this treasonous affair. He needed to find Commander Camdus fast, but first he needed to try to revive Dormax and the Enright woman. He set his weapon to shock and delivered one to the shoulder of Dormax. Nothing. He shocked him again, this time on the left chest. Dormax dropped from his rigid state.

Grunden bent down to check his vitals. Thankfully, his eyes had adjusted just enough for him to see his surroundings. Dormax looked and started to speak but Grunden shushed him, pointing to the REG emblem on his uniform.

Grunden whispered, "Dormax?"

The dazed man replied, "Yes. How did you know?"

Grunden grunted, "Lucky guess. Who's the woman?" Dormax told him the woman's name, Rayalla. He said that they had been captured and brought here several weeks ago — first, the men, then the woman.

He went on to ask, "Is it over?"

Grunden looked at the man harder, trying to discern his meaning. "Is what over?" he demanded.

The man fell silent. Grunden shook him. "Look, I didn't come here to be lied to or misdirected again. If you want out of here, you damn well better tell me what you know - now." Dormax began by telling Grunden that he had been threatened into helping Weilz, the Prime Minister, to steal some very valuable documents regarding troop deployments. He said that Weilz had promised not to harm him or his family if he cooperated. But Weilz had lied. Oh yes, Weilz had given him a pod to get away in and he had used it to go home to his see family again to reassure himself that they were all right. Dormax had planned to stay with them for a while then move on as quietly as he could. But after only a week, Weilz had sent the mercenary Serin to his father's home. Though he and his dad had resisted, they had been no match for him. He had immobilized them both and kidnapped them.

They woke up in this place, called Q'Door Hold. At first they were allowed to live fairly well in rather nice quarters, even having access to an illuminated "courtyard" where they took afternoon walks. But then about a week ago, they were summoned to the old man Elsnor's quarters. After a brief interview, Elsnor had looked at them and smiled.

"That was the last thing I remember until just now when you woke me. Can you wake my father, also?"

Grunden now knew Dormax's family had lied, but shocked his father back to consciousness. He then asked about the woman.

"I've told you all I know about her – her name is Rayalla."

Grunden left Dormax tending to his father and moved to the woman. He set his weapon at the lowest level possible as she was of slight build. She woke instantly, and stood blinking into the dark. He had expected her to panic, but she didn't. She reached out to him, felt his face, and then dropped her hand. "I thought you might be someone else," she whispered and fell silent again.

Just as Grunden was about to speak, he heard a soft popping sound. Rax had appeared from nowhere. "Commander Camdus is in need of your assistance, Mr. Grunden. He has sent me to bring you to him."

Grunden looked at the totally nonplussed Rax. "Listen Rax, you've got to go back to the Commander and tell him we have found Dormax, his father, and Enright's sister. I need him here to help us figure this mess out. Can you do that?" Rax nodded, and with another soft pop, disappeared.

Within a minute, Rax and Camdus both appeared in the now crowded closet. Camdus did not speak, but reached for the woman. She stepped close to him and as with Grunden felt his face. She released a low sigh and fell into his arms. He held her to him, gently stroking her hair. "Rayalla" was the only word he said.

Grunden cleared his throat, "Commander, we have a situation here. I'm not sure where we are, but this prisoner hold seems to be fairly safe – at least for the moment. Now the problem is how do we get them out of here?"

Cam instantly let go of the woman and took on his role of Commander. "I can get them out. Rax, take them back to the pods. Then back to the ship. When they're safely aboard, return to me, wherever I am. Understood?" Rax nodded, encircled the three captives in his very long arms, and with a pop, transported them to the pod. Within half an hour, the pod was back at the mother ship where the captives were taken to the infirmary. The pod was returned to Creedor, and hidden along with the other pods to await the landing party's return.

Camdus and Grunden find Elsnor

When Rax popped back in on Commander Camdus, Grunden and the others had moved to a storage area behind what looked like the maintenance room for the transport tube.

". . . to get to whoever is running this place, Commander. We can't just free the slaves and leave," Grunden was saying when Rax returned.

"I have no intention of leaving without finishing the job, Mr. Grunden. But you do remember that our initial mission is to end the epidemic. Jarlod has yet to respond to my request for more troops to squelch this invasion, so it looks like it's on us."

Camdus then addressed all the men, "I don't want to order you to stay with me, but if I have to, I will. I wish I could release you from this mission, but I can't. Even so, I need to know that you are here because you take this responsibility, along with the danger it brings, as seriously as I do." He waited, watching his soldiers carefully. He had to know that he could still depend on each man.

They straightened in unison, saluting their Commander. Grunden spoke for them. "Sir, we're not cowards. We're in, whether you order us or not." Stad and Ram knew they could walk away and the Commander couldn't do anything about it, but once a soldier, always a soldier. So they stood with the soldiers, just as determined to win this fight or die trying.

Cam looked each man straight in the eye for confirmation. Satisfied, he gave his first order, "All right, then. First we need to find the headquarters. I know we're near it;

I just don't know where it is. I've heard them, and have seen two of their beasts. I'm not sure what happened to one of them, but for the last few hours, there's been only one down here. Not knowing where one of them is hiding is worse than knowing where this one is. Stadar, Ram. What do you two know about this part of Q'Door Hold?" Stadar knew nothing of it and said so. Ram had been to the tower once, when Li'Let had left him alone for a while. The harrowing ride on the transport tube had taken at least a few years off his life, he was sure. From his hiding place in a seldom used stairwell, he had watched various people coming and going from two huge doors at the end of the hallway. Li'Let had been one of them. There was also a tall man with long black hair dressed completely in black which made him look quite sinister. The most interesting one was an older gentleman dressed in royal blue. His bald head stuck strangely out of the thin fringe of snow white hair that flowed halfway down his back. Others stepped aside when he approached. Ram related this to Grunden and Cam, who exchanged glances.

Cam's concern was plain – "So Elsnor is in charge. He has powers at least equal to if not greater than Vandalen of Trilvar. And, Grunden, I think that he is the one you saw talking to Slogar. We've got to bring the doctor here immediately. Rax, if you please." Without a word, Rax disappeared with his signature pop. "We'll get to the bottom of this when the good doctor returns. Meanwhile, we need to find out where Serin is. That's the tall man dressed in black, Ramar. It's very fortunate for you that you didn't cross his path." Ram felt a slight shiver down his spine; once again he had been spared.

After a bit, Rax popped back alone. "I'm sorry, Commander. The doctor was not able to join you," he said as casually as if talking of attending an afternoon tea. "I see. Well then, Rax. Take me to him."With that, they were gone. Grunden thought this was as good an opportunity as any to check out this part of Q'Door Hold. He started to step out of their hiding place, but Ramar pulled him back. "I know I'm no longer in the REG, but Mr. Grunden, I know more about Q'Door Hold. Halfway between dusk and dawn there's hardly anyone in the corridors I've been on. I don't know where they go or what they do, but they're not in the passageways."

Grunden interrupted, "That sounds like the safest time for us to move."

Ramar agreed, but registered his concern, "Unfortunately, that is when the big cats roam freely."

Grunden knew it was too good to be true. "Okay, then. What do you know about the cats?"

Ram replied, "Well, for one thing, the female can read minds when in human form. I don't think she can when she changes. When she hunted me in the maze, she did so by animal instinct and her animal senses. If she could read minds then, she should have been able to find me in my hiding places. She always sniffled and pawed around the maze, sometimes so close I held my breath. But she would growl and go on." Grunden knew about the beasts, but he was pretty sure that one of them was no longer in Q'Door Hold. If it was, then it had changed shapes again.

Before they could further explore this dilemma, Rax popped back in with Camdus. Then popped out and back with Slogar. His face was purple from the strain of holding on to his cargo; Slogar had gained weight – again. Rax gratefully released him and sat down on the floor to catch his breath.

Camdus surveyed the group before going on. "We may have to redirect our efforts; the epidemic is worsening by the minute. The good doctor here is in need of help from the Elder Woman of Silden, but he will have to go to her."

Slogar was really eager to be on his way, especially to see Elani again. But now he knew that he might have information that Camdus needed to fight the Q'Arons. So he had agreed to come here first to meet with the Commander and his men. Grunden got straight to the point, "Tell me, Doctor, who was the Trilvarian you met with on Boldoon at the Boor's Nad Inn before the Commander contacted you?" Slogar knew this day would come; now he had no choice but to be truthful, no matter what.

"That, my dear Mr. Grunden, was none other than Vandalen of Trilvar."

Camdus and Grunden looked at Slogar in disbelief. Cam said emphatically, "Come off it, Slogar. That's simply not possible. There is no way that Vandalen could have escaped Dartal."

"I beg to differ. Jarlod never knew the instrument of the wizard's power. Everyone assumed it was the ring. But it wasn't; the ring was one of twelve. Only charter members of an ancient wizard fraternity have them. And it is true, that with the rings, the wizards' powers were amplified. But the root of their power is within them; they need nothing to facilitate its use. All Vandalen ever had to do was think what he wanted or where he wanted to go, and it was as he thought. Vandalen is a peaceful man; he served Elder Borm because he was benevolent. The Elder's kindness was mistaken as weakness by many, but Van knew and he served willingly. When Jarlod overthrew Borm, Vandalen refused to serve him, for he could see into the heart of the man and what he saw was evil."

Cam had been listening carefully, but was growing tired of not having Grunden's question answered. "So Vandalen was good; Jarlod was bad. I get that. What were you and he talking about at the Boor's Nad Inn?"

Slogar took a deep breath. "We were talking about a coup. There is, and has been for quite some time a movement among certain groups to remove Jarlod from power before he completely destroys the Empire. Vandalen was trying to recruit me. He said that when the time came, there would be need for learned men who could not only teach, but also do. I laughed out loud, as I recall. It had been so long since anyone had taken me seriously, or even remembered me at all. I thought he was poking fun at me, just like regulars at the Inn. But after outlining how far he'd come already toward putting his plan in motion, I knew he was serious. I listened, but politely declined. You saw me, Cam. I was an ale junkie with no further ambition than to swill drink and eat myself sick. Hell, if you hadn't gotten me out of my funk when you did, I have no doubt I'd be dead by now. And you may not believe it, but when I was with Seelah and Elani, I actually lost weight and had a clear head. She's not going to be happy to see the way I've let myself go."

Camdus stopped his ramblings, "So you know how to contact Vandalen?"

"I didn't contact him; he found me. But I know who can contact him – his daughter, Elani."

"You're kidding me, right? You spent all that time with Vandalen's daughter and you didn't think that was important enough to tell me?" Camdus was really ticked now. He had stepped closer to Slogar and was speaking in that low tone that every man who'd ever served under him knew; and they didn't have time for that.

Grunden stepped between the men, "Look, Commander, let's step back a minute. Remember, the doctor is under the Emperor's protection." Any other time and Camdus would have disciplined Grunden for his insolence, but he needed every man. And, to be honest with himself, he needed to cool down. Decisions made in anger were seldom wise.

"One more question, Doctor. If Vandalen could 'think' himself free, then why did he go back to Dartal?" Camdus knew an inconsistency when he heard one.

"His daughter. Jarlod threatened to add her to his harem. Though Van's power without the ring allowed him to travel, it was not enough to protect Elani. Believe it or not, the great wizard gave up his freedom for nothing more than sentiment." Camdus was still skeptical, but knew that this was not the time to delve into the matter. He hoped that he would not regret this decision.

They were fairly certain that at least two things had to happen: Slogar had to go back to the plains of Silden, and then he had to convince Elani to contact her father so that she could solicit his help. Camdus instructed Grunden and the others to keep a low profile, but to gather as much information as possible. They knew they would need provisions; with the Rider in their midst, that was not a problem.

Camdus instinctively felt that now was the time to open the small package his father had given him before he left for the academy. He had placed it in a small tredon leather pouch and worn it as a talisman of sorts, but had never felt the need to open it – until now. Stepping away from the group as they continued to strategize, he opened his father's gift. Inside he found a collection of small items. One was a ring. Camdus was dumbfounded as he stared at the ring which was exactly like that of Vandalen and Elsnor. He placed it on his finger. He felt an intense sensation of power pulsing through his body. He quickly took the ring off. What was this? The ring was supposed to hold no special powers, yet clearly this one did. He put it back on his finger. Again he felt the pulsating sensation. He intuited many things that were unknown to him before. He knew now more than ever that he had to find Vandalen. He also had many questions for his father, but they would have to wait. He took the ring off yet again and put it back in the pouch. Next he found a tiny button-like device. He had no idea what it was. Okay. He pulled out the ring and placed it on his finger once again. Instantly he knew what to do with this button. It was a cloaking device that could be used to protect the group until he and Slogar returned, hopefully with Vandalen. He stepped back into the midst of the men as they continued to brainstorm.

Camdus cleared his throat, "Mr. Grunden, a word please." Grunden looked away from Stadar, who had been describing the inhabitants of Q'Door Hold.

"Yes, Commander?"

Camdus indicated that he wanted to speak to him in private, so they both stepped away. The others paid little attention, for each had something to offer to the discussion.

He placed the button in Grunden's hand. "Just touch the back of this button and a perception baffle will be created to hide your location. To disengage, just hold it 10 seconds."

"Where did this come from, Commander? I've never even heard of anything like this."

Camdus replied, honestly, "It was a gift. But now the doctor and I have to go. Take care of the men. We'll be back as soon as possible. Rax will be back after he delivers us to Silden."

Grunden saluted, "God go with you, Commander."

"And you as well, Mr. Grunden." With that, Camdus summoned Rax, who took a deep breath and held on to both the Commander and Slogar. In a split second they were gone.

The Elder Woman Helps Out

Rax brought them to the porch of the old shack on the plains. Commander Camdus thanked him and sent him back to Q'Door Hold. Rax was sweating profusely and completely winded. As soon as he could stand straight again, he nodded and was gone in an instant.

"All right, Doctor. Lead the way." Slogar dreaded the wobbly steps but knew that Seelah and Elani were below in the elaborate underground facility. He held onto the porch rail to steady himself and made his way up the steps. In two strides, he was inside. It was as he remembered it, but this time Seelah was standing in full regalia by the hearth.

"Why, Simon. So good of you to come. And this must be Commander Camdus. Welcome, Commander." Cam didn't know how she knew his name but was not surprised. Slogar had told him about his time here, so nothing much would surprise him.

"Thank you for having us, Elder Woman." When she smiled, her blue eyes twinkled. Camdus noticed that she was a tall woman who bore herself with a sense of knowing. He wondered how much she knew.

"Come, Gentlemen. Elani and I have been expecting you."

"Seelah," Slogar asked, "you didn't will us here, did you?" Now she laughed that cathartic laugh that he realized suddenly how much he'd missed.

"Not this time. But your coming was made known to us. Let's go below where you can rest a bit before supper." She laid one hand on the mantel and one on Slogar, who laid his hand on Camdus' shoulder. Slogar was prepared for this particular mode of transport and the disinfectant mist, but had forgotten to warn Camdus.

"What the...?" Camdus sputtered after he found his legs again.

"Oh, yeah," Slogar offered, "I forgot to tell you about how we get back and forth from the surface to below. Sorry."

Cam shot the doctor a look that made Slogar thankful that a lady was present. He was grateful for the ointment Seelah had used to stop his eyes from burning.

Seelah summoned Elani. When she saw Slogar, her eyes lit with fondness. "Elani, please take Simon to his room. I wish to speak to Commander Camdus a moment; I'll show him to his room myself."

Elani replied, "As you wish, Ma'am." She and Slogar disappeared down the long hall to the guest rooms.

Seelah invited Camdus to sit. A porcelain pot of thistle tea was on the table between them, steam pouring from its delicately curved spout. She leaned over and poured a cup and handed it to him. Then she poured one for herself. The warm tea steadied his still spinning head.

"Thank you, Elder Woman. You no doubt know that this is not a social call?"

Seelah replied, "Yes, I am aware. Please, Commander, call me Seelah. I feel quite ancient when addressed by my title."

Camdus realized the faux pas, and immediately apologized. "Please forgive me, Seelah. I never intended to offend. I was unsure of the proper…"

Seelah interrupted, "No apology needed, Commander. We have more important issues at hand." Camdus was impressed by his gracious hostess; he could see that she must have been a striking beauty as a young woman for she was a lovely, graceful elder. Letting him off the hook for his fumble also impressed him and put him at ease.

"Then thank you, Seelah. How much do you know of our reasons for coming here?"

"I know that you are in need of Elani's assistance because you need Vandalen." Seelah continued, "I also know that you have left some of you soldiers on Creedor and that they may be in danger. Beyond that, I'm afraid I am in the dark."

Camdus wondered if Seelah was ever really in the dark, but she had given no reason to doubt her.

"Seelah, we do need to contact Vandalen. Elsnor, another Trilvarian wizard, is in league with the Q'Arons. We know they have kidnapped many of the Creedorian citizens and are using them as slaves in the trizactl mining operation they've set up on Creedor. We also know that they are, whether they know it or not, part of a plot to overthrow Jarlod."

At this Seelah indulged in a rare scornful laugh. "Which one?"

Camdus realized that she did indeed know more about what was going on than he had given her credit for. "What do you mean, 'which one'? How many are there?"

Seelah sat back sipping her tea. "Commander, you do know, of course, I only have knowledge of some things, not everything?" Seelah waited for Cam's nod of understanding before continuing.

"Well then, let's see. Elsnor wishes to become an Emperor himself; a group of Boldoonian rebels want to take power, but have no clear plan of who the Emperor should be,..." Cam knew very well which group she was referring to. "...but they are reacting to the maltreatment they have endured. They have been overly cautious, and without a solid plan. I'm quite sure they are stepping out on faith, to borrow a phrase, that the proper leader will rise to the top. There are so many problems with that; but I digress. Then there is Weilz who has hungered for the Emperor's power since he was appointed Prime Minister, ungrateful dog that he is. One could say that our Emperor has made many enemies and even those he perceives to be friends are of the fair weather variety."

Camdus had listened carefully to Seelah's analysis of the Emperor's enemies. He knew she was right; he only hoped that there were no other groups to contend with. "You are very astute, Seelah. I have the Boldoonians under my control currently, so that is one less to worry about. But of the other two, which do you feel is the greatest threat?"

Without a pause, Seelah answered, "Elsnor."

Cam echoed her assessment, "I think you're right. He seems to have extraordinary powers. Some of my men have seen him. They say that everyone around him bows to him whenever he enters a room or corridor. I don't get how Elsnor's gotten the Q'Arons, who are barbaric at best, to give him obeisance. He must have enchanted them." Seelah pondered this as she poured more tea for herself and offered more to Camdus, who declined.

Seelah responded thoughtfully, "I'm not so sure that it is enchantment he uses. He was never the strongest wizard of the twelve. But he was the hungriest for power. I dare say he is using his powers to torture the Q'Arons into submission. He has never figured out that real power is benevolent."

Seelah and Camdus sat quietly for a moment, the Elder Woman sipping her tea; Camdus deep in thought.

After a bit, Seelah put down her cup and said, "Come with me, Commander. I can see how tired you are. Your room is just down this hall." Camdus realized that he was past tired and thankfully followed the Elder Woman. She stopped at a door that had his name on it; inside was what looked like the room from the happiest time of his life. He half expected to see his mother there tidying his things as she had done when he still lived at home. "Seelah, I don't know how you've done this, but thank you."

Seelah just smiled, "You're welcome, Commander. Elani will escort you to supper in an hour." Camdus turned to find that clean clothes had been laid out for him. He also saw that he had something here he had not had at home: a private bath and walk-in changing area. He gratefully stepped into the bathing area and warmed his weary muscles in the steaming shower. It was such a relief to get the smell of disinfectant off his body. He dressed in the clean uniform, made of the finest tredon leather he noted, and waited for Elani to fetch him for supper.

Camdus didn't have long to wait as Elani knocked on his door within a few minutes of his settling down to read one of the magazines he remembered from his youth. Seelah clearly had extraordinary powers, but not the kind he thought they needed for this fight. He stepped out into the hall and greeted Elani, who smiled acknowledgment and strode ahead of him.

"Elani, please may I have a word with you?" She stopped and looked back at him, waiting for him to catch up.

"Of course, Commander," she answered. Camdus had no idea how to broach the subject of her father, but decided to be direct.

"Elani, I understand that you are the daughter of the wizard Vandalen. Is that correct?" She looked at him, cautious now, but nodded affirmatively.

"Can you contact him for me? I, no, we need his help. But I especially need his help with a project that is integral to our plan." Elani had not yet spoken, and truly was at a loss for words. How long had it been since she had spoken to her father. He had left her and her mother and brother to pursue his career. And for what? To allow himself to become a prisoner on bleak Dartal? She had spent many years brooding over her father's seeming abandonment of her. But now, with Seelah's help and wisdom, she had at last forgiven him and perhaps begun to understand a bit better the position he had been placed in by Elder Borm. Seelah knew that Elder Borm had touted Vandalen as an almighty wizard, though he considered himself no more than a man with a gift who had learned to make science and physics work for him. And yes, he had mastered the techniques necessary to channel various types of energy and make it do his will. There was none greater than he, at least not in Seelah's telling of the story to Elani. And as Seelah had hoped, Elani's anger melted. In its place was a longing to see her father, to tell him what was in her heart. But she had thought that was not possible. But now Commander Camdus was standing beside her, asking her to contact him.

She spoke softly, "Commander, it has never occurred to me that I might be able to do that without help of a Rider." Even as she spoke her heart leapt with joy. Commander Camdus had a Rider under his command. Rax would surely take her to her father.

"Elani, tell me you can ask your father to help us, and I'll have Rax here in a matter of moments."

She took a deep breath, "Yes, Commander, I can summon my father, but I must go with the Rider, if we are to have any hope of his assistance. But now we must be on our way. The Elder Woman is waiting for us to join her for dinner; Doctor Slogar is already there. We will talk to her about this after dinner." Camdus breathed a sigh of relief. Now, to get them into and out of the Dartal prison without detection would require planning. He would need a little time to gather some information before he allowed Elani and Rax to try it; that is, if Seelah approved. He knew one thing for sure: he was hungry and whatever was on the menu made his mouth water.

Conversation during the meal was light and very enjoyable; Camdus felt that it would be rude to broach the subject that needed to be addressed so he waited patiently. After a perfectly prepared meal of white fish with a lovely salad from Elani's garden, Seelah invited them to join her in her larger sitting room. The flames, pink and gold this evening, gave a warmth to the otherwise austere room. Once seated, she served tea with candied fruit compote for dessert. Camdus sat back in his chair, savoring the wonderful flavors.

"This is really good, Seelah." Seelah, never one to take undue credit, made sure he knew that all meals were the result of Elani's talents.

"Then, Elani, I thank you; I can't remember when I've eaten so well." Elani smiled shyly and nodded her acceptance of his praise. Slogar had enjoyed the meal, but Cam thought that perhaps he was enjoying seeing Elani even more.

Putting these simple thoughts aside, Camdus spoke. "Seelah, I am in need of Elani's help. I've asked her to summon her father, as I feel that she may be the only one who can. But," he went on, looking at Elani, "she wants to go to Dartal with Rax to get him. How do you feel about that?"

The calm expression of the seasoned hostess was ruffled for a split second, but then returned to its normal placid state. "Commander, this sounds like a very dangerous task for Elani to undertake. Why can't she summon him and wait here for him to join her?"

"I know what you're saying, Seelah. That was my original request of her; but Elani said that she has to go with Rax. I would prefer her to stay here, but whatever it takes, so be it. I mean, if that's what she thinks it'll take to get him to help us, then I think it's worth the risk," Camdus said bluntly.

Seelah moved her gaze from Camdus to Elani. For the first time, she saw a fire in her charge. "Elani, my dear, are you quite aware of the danger you will be putting yourself in to accomplish this task? You could be seriously injured, or worse. Elani, is it worth it to speak to your father again?"

Elani answered firmly and with no hesitation, "Yes, Ma'am. I am well aware of the risks. But ever since coming here with you, I have had time to consider the relationship with my father and let the hurt heal. I need for my father to know that his daughter is okay. More than that, I want him to know that I love him unconditionally. I want to go, Elder Woman. I am asking your blessing, but know that I feel compelled to go without it if I must."

Tears shimmered on Elani's lashes, touching Seelah's heart. She rose from her seat at the head of the table and went to Elani. Elani stood to face her, not knowing what to expect. Seelah enfolded her in a tender embrace, holding her for a moment.

Then she let her go, stood back, placed a hand on her head, "God be with you, Elani. I trust we'll be together again soon." Elani was elated. Feeling a bit lightheaded with relief, she turned to Camdus.

"When do we leave, Commander?" With one hurdle cleared, Camdus asked Seelah to help him with the logistics for Rax and Elani's mission. They excused themselves to Seelah's study, leaving Slogar and Elani alone in the dining room. Throughout the evening, Slogar had been unusually quiet.

"Elani, I . . .," he began. She placed a slender finger over his lips. "Simon, please don't say it. You know I have to do what is in my heart."

The look on his face spoke to her spirit. "Oh, Simon. Yes, you too are in my heart, but this is different. I have an inexplicable need to find my father and make things right with him again. For so long, I blamed him for the ills in my life. Only after much time with Seelah was I able to see that my perception was not necessarily the way things really were. He is in prison, but he should not be there; I know that beyond all doubt."

Slogar took her hand. "Elani, I have no reason to ever hope that you could ever consider me as a partner to travel with through this life, and yet, I do. I am so much older than you, and look at me; I'm surely not a 'catch' as they say. But Elani, you have stolen something that used to be mine. And I do not want it back." He stopped talking, embarrassed at his schoolboy gushing. Who was this idiot residing within him, anyway? He was slamming himself, when he realized that Elani was laughing softly first, then out loud. "Simon, you are so funny. You think you're older than I am? Do you have any idea how old I am?" Slogar just shook his head no. "Let's just say that I was in the fullness of my season when you were born. So Simon, how do you feel about older women?" His embrace and gentle kiss told her it didn't matter at all.

But stepping back, he said, "Elani, all my life I hoped for someone to share my dreams. I can't abide the thought that now I've found you, you may not return to me. Please don't go."

Elani knew how he felt; she felt it too. But she had made up her mind. "Simon, pray for my safety. I will return to you. And when I do, we're going to whip you into shape; we will continue our evening walks and oh yes, our fishing. You still have your destiny to fulfill, and I want you to be healthy enough to do it. Do you agree?"

He was so taken aback by this whole revelation, he quietly said, "If you say so, then yes."

Camdus and Seelah were working in the study when Slogar and Elani joined them. "Well, what've you come up with, Commander?" Slogar asked as they entered the room.

Seelah looked up from the hologram that stood glimmering atop the table. "This is the prison on Dartal, and here ..." Camdus indicated the far tower, "is where Vandalen is being kept. His night guards are not as diligent as those during the day. Even though Rax can pop in and out fairly quickly, he is not invincible. One good nucleo blast would be devastating to the cause." Seelah raised her brow, "Hmmm. I'm fairly sure that it would not very good for Rax, either." Camdus took the reprimand in stride. "Of course, Seelah. However, at this point, we never know when any one or all of us will be in harm's way. All we can do is try to make sure we execute each maneuver as precisely as possible. Elani, are you quite sure I can't talk you out of this mission? Rax can have your father back in a very short time, so you really don't have to go. I just need you to send him a message."

Elani listened carefully, but Slogar recognized that look. There was no backing out; there would be no more waiting. "I appreciate your concern, Commander, but I will go with Rax. When can we leave?"

Cam knew when he was fighting a losing battle, so conceded with, "Tonight, around midnight seems to be the perfect time, based on our data. I will summon Rax two hours before your departure. I want to make sure he is well versed in all the details of the mission. And I want you to wear a tredon battle uniform and helmet. They will offer pretty substantial protection. Do you have access to one?" Seelah assured him she would see to Elani's outfitting.

"Do you have a weapon? You may need one, you know." Elani had never needed a weapon before, but trusted the Commander's judgment. Seelah pulled a mini nucleo from the folds of her robe and handed it to Camdus. Surprised, but pleased, he said, "Perfect. Now, Elani. Is there a place where I can teach you how to use it?" Elani knew the exact location for them to practice.

"Come with me, Commander." Elani led him from the room to a large empty space one level down. "Will this do?" Camdus marveled at the intricacies of this facility. After about half an hour, they returned to the group, with Elani relieved to have attained at least a competency that might save their lives, if need be.

At midnight, Elani and Rax stood silently together, Rax' arms securely wrapped around Elani, who showed no emotion on her face. With a last "God speed" from Seelah, they popped out.

Vandalen joins the fight

The wizard was not asleep, but lay looking up at the spider dangling from a silken thread attached to the ceiling above. He had found countless ways to keep his mind alert, including trying to calculate the number of times the spider swung from left to right. Three hundred and fourteen, three hundred and fifteen, three hu . . . . A soft pop in the darkest corner of his cell caught his attention. He was instantly on his feet, ready to fight. He saw a girl and a very tall man standing there. Now Vandalen questioned whether his mental exercises had backfired on him.

"Father," the girl said in a soft whisper as she stepped toward him. He relaxed his stance only a little. How could this be? Was it possible that this was the young girl he had left at home all those years ago? He was afraid this was another trick, but after looking at her for a long moment he knew that before him stood his only daughter.

"Elani? How did you get here? Your mother, your brother, are they...?"

Elani touched her finger to her lips and stepped close to his ear, "Father, we will have time later to speak; now Rax and I need you to come with us." Vandalen was trying to take this in. How could he be really sure this wasn't another one of Elsnor's tricks?

"All right, Elani. I'll go with you, but where are we going?" Elani spoke softer still, "Silden." With that, they stepped into the shadows with Rax. With his daughter safely beside him, Vandalen was finally free of Dartal.

Seelah, Slogar, and Camdus sat silently in the parlor. The air was electric with anticipation. Slogar was in the middle of what seemed to him like an endless prayer when Rax and his charges popped back in. and his charges popped back in. Camdus was the first to greet them. He rose calmly, thanked Rax, and released him to return to Q'Door Hold. But Seelah interrupted, "Please wait a moment, Rax." He looked at his commander for affirmation. Camdus nodded, so Rax waited. In a very short time, Seelah returned with a large package filled with provisions for Rax and the soldiers at Q'Door Hold.

"Thank you, Ma'am," Rax said and with package securely wrapped in his long arms, obeyed the Commander's order to return to Q'Door Hold.

Next Camdus turned to Elani and Vandalen; the resemblance was striking. How could he have not seen that before?

Elani walked to Slogar and gently touched his arm. "Simon, will you join me for a walk? I see that Father and the Commander have work to do."

"Of course, my dear. But don't you need to eat first?" Elani looked at him, and once again he read the gaze.

"Very well then," Slogar said. "Seelah, Gentlemen, we'll be in the garden if you need us."

After Elani and Slogar left, Camdus spoke to Vandalen respectfully, "Sir, thank you for agreeing to help us. We have much to do." Seelah led them to her study where the hologram now present was of Q'Door Hold.

Vandalen looked from the hologram to Camdus and then spoke for the first time. "I'm not sure that I've agreed to anything yet. My daughter asked me to come with her, so I did. What do you want from me, Commander?" Seelah brought a platter of leftover tredon steaks and hard rolls. She offered tea, which both men declined.

"Do you have anything stronger?"Vandalen asked. Seelah placed a carafe of wine on the table and sat down beside them, pouring herself a cup of steaming thistle tea. Vandalen greedily laid into the food. But he listened as Camdus briefed him.

"Your fellow wizard Elsnor has joined forces with our enemies, the Q'Arons. They've been stealing trizactl from Creedor, but they've also released a deadly plague to eliminate any of the citizens left topside. The rest have been enslaved in the mines or are being held in Q'Door Hold. Jarlod refuses to pull his head out of the sand long enough to realize that we're in a hell of a lot of trouble. We need reinforcements, which he has yet to provide."

Vandalen had finished stuffing himself, at least for the moment. He drained a goblet of wine, and then spoke again. "Elsnor? That sorry excuse for a wizard. The Council expelled him for unethical use of his powers. We tried to retrieve the ring, but he vanished before we could."

Camdus took mention of the ring to get to the real reason he needed to talk to Vandalen. He pulled the pouch from his shirt and pulled out the ring his father had given him. "Was it like this one?" Vandalen looked at the object in Camdus' hand. Vandalen asked to examine it.

Camdus did not yet fully trust the wizard, so he said to him, "First let me tell you what happens when I put the ring on."

When Camdus had finished, Vandalen was speechless for a moment, then replied, "Well, for one thing, I now know that you are Willem's true son for that is Willem's ring and only one of his blood could experience any of its power. So why did he pass it along while still able to use it? I can only speculate. Will was one of the best of us, until he met a certain young woman, who was ignorant of his heritage. He gave up his seat on the Council, but we asked him to keep his ring for there might come a time when his gifts would be needed."

Vandalen realized from the look on the commander's face that he had never been told any of this. "I'm sorry if I've spoken out of school; I thought you knew at least some of it."

Camdus thought of how to ask the next question. "So are you saying that my father is a wizard and that I am, too?" Vandalen nodded, but followed with a warning. "You are inexperienced with the powers of the ring. But you must know that the ring is powerless unless worn by the wizard born to wear it, or his heir. When an old wizard dies without an heir, the ring becomes a pretty bauble. You also need to know that just because you have a talent or gift doesn't mean you know how to use it properly. One last thing, for some wizards the thrill of the power overcomes their self-control."

"Like Elsnor?" Camdus asked.

"Exactly like Elsnor," Vandalen replied.

Camdus set down his wine goblet, the new information about his father and himself swirling in his brain. "Then teach me," he said to Vandalen as he poured a cup of thistle tea. He didn't want fuzzy thinking to screw with his mastering this new tool.

Vandalen considered the request. "Why should I, Commander?"

Camdus looked squarely at him, "Your daughter is in just as much danger as the rest of us. Once they finish with Creedor, how long do you think it will be before the Q'Arons locate this facility?"

The truth of Camdus' words hit its mark. "Do we have time for a short rest? I'm exhausted."

Camdus offered his room, but Seelah, who had been quietly listening to this conversation, now spoke, "Vandalen, you have a room of your own. I'll show you to it, if you're ready." Camdus should have known. The Elder Woman always had a room for her visitors. Vandalen gladly accepted her offer.

"Commander," Seelah said as they were parting, "perhaps you should take advantage of this time to rest also. You will need all your strength and energy for what's to come." Camdus got the feeling that somehow Seelah had an idea of what that was, but he knew better than to ask. He was certain Seelah would tell him what he needed to know when the time was right. He took one more sip of his tea; then he retired for a few hours of much needed rest.

Seelah's knocking on his door woke Camdus after what seemed like only a few minutes. "Commander, it will be daylight soon. Breakfast is ready. Please join us." Daylight! He should have been up and ready by now. No sense beating himself up over it; what was done was done. He rushed to cleanup and pack what he knew he'd need for his journey. He made sure his father's pouch was hanging securely around his neck and hidden beneath his uniform. He raced down the long hallway back to the dining area. His first reaction was relief to find that he was not the last to arrive. That, however, was rapidly followed by a sense of disappointment that his tutor was not there yet. "Vandalen?" His one word question was answered by Seelah.

"He will be here momentarily. He was preparing for your lessons today. Ah, here he is now. Good morning, Vandalen. I hope you slept well." Vandalen had not been surprised to find the room a replica of his own. He knew that Seelah had great powers, though limited to the plains of Silden. 'Pity,' he thought, 'we could surely use her skills.'

He took his place at the table and was very pleased to see his daughter at the table. "Elani, how have you been?"

Elani looked at her father, her anger long gone. "I've had a good life here with Seelah; before she took me in, not so much. But that is hardly fit conversation for the breakfast table. I will be glad when this terrible business is complete; then we will have all the time in the world to catch up."

Elani's father took the answer in stride, but pressed with the two questions he'd tried to ask last evening. "How is your mother? She was so distressed when I was imprisoned."

"Mother has passed on to the next realm, Father. She loved you for all her life, but the loneliness was more than she could bear."

Vandalen felt as if a knife had been thrust into his heart, but pressed on. "And your brother? How is Serin?"

Camdus nearly fell out of his chair. "Serin is your son!? Do you know what he's become? Soldier, assassin. Whatever his employer is willing to pay him to do."

Elani looked as if someone had slapped her; she was well aware of her brother's profession, but had hoped to be able to spare her father the pain she knew that knowledge would cause him.

"Commander! Please, let's not discuss this now. Perhaps later, but not now." Seelah's voice was firm, but Camdus would not be stopped.

Camdus roared, "No. We're going to get this out now. He is at Q'Door Hold, working for Elsnor, no doubt. What am I supposed to do — sit back and give him a pass because of his family? Hell no! He never cared about the families of those he harmed, and..."

Seelah said once again, this time in a low, menacing tone, "Commander, I'm warning you. Do not go there again. I said later, and I meant it. But now we have to find a way to rescue him."

"Rescue a murderer? No disrespect, but have you lost your mind, Seelah? I'm sitting here wondering how many of my men he's harmed at Q'Door Hold, and you're sitting here feeling sorry for him?!" Camdus stopped, absolutely speechless.

Seelah replied, "Commander, you don't know if that's true. And even if it is, as long as there's life, there's hope for redemption. Now let's drop this and eat."

Camdus rose from the table and walked out of the room. 'What the ...,' his thoughts raced, 'am I in some parallel universe where truth is lie and bad is good?' He had been aimlessly walking and soon rounded a curve in the concourse revealing, of all things, a vast ocean with trees, beaches, birds; everything he'd remembered from the shores of his youth. He walked down the beach a bit before sitting down on the warm sand. He lay back and soaked in the warmth of the sand and sun. Right now he wished he knew the power of the ring so that he could find out for himself if Seelah was right.

At that moment, a shadow fell across him, blocking the sun. "Commander, it is time for our lesson." Vandalen had followed him, knowing that he had to save his son, no matter what. But he did not want to become ruthless to do it; perhaps he could instruct Camdus in the tools associated with his heritage and together they could discover the truth about his son. He knew, as a seasoned wizard and soldier, that even good men can go bad. But he had hope that Serin was ready to remember his birthright and mend his ways. Otherwise, well he just did not want to think about that – not unless he had to.

Camdus got up and faced Vandalen. "You're right, Vandalen. I will trust Seelah's wisdom and your experience in these things. And for your and Elani's sake, I pray that your son has changed."

The men walked back to the room where Camdus had given Elani her weapons lesson. "Will this do?" Vandalen thought it quite suited to his purposes.

"Yes, it's as good a place as any, better than most. May I now hold your ring?" Camdus pulled the ring out of the pouch and handed it to the wizard. Vandalen held it in his hand. Of course, he felt none of its power as it was crafted for Willem Camdus and his heirs. But his examination revealed that this was indeed a genuine wizard ring. He needed for Camdus to help him get back his own ring.

"First you will learn to calm the confusion you feel when the power courses through you as you wear the ring. Otherwise, it will consume you. To do that, you have to breathe deeply and evenly. Don't let the excitement of having this much power run away with your common sense. It truly is a matter of mental fortitude. Are you ready?"

Camdus had been ready, but now he hesitated. "What will happen if I can't control it?" Vandalen smiled.

"You've worn the ring before, correct?" Vandalen's question registered through the doubts.

"Yes, I have. It was exhilarating, but scary. I took it off after only a few moments each time."

Vandalen listened; then he asked, "Were you able to wear it for longer periods the more you wore it?"

Camdus admitted that he had, adding, "And each time the power seemed stronger, more organized. But was it organizing itself, or was I? I need to know."

The wizard was relieved to hear this. "The power knows no discipline. So if it was organized, then you were in control of it. Now put the ring on. Please." Camdus placed the ring on his right index finger. The now familiar feeling flooded his body so strongly that he snatched it off. "Put the ring back on, Commander. This time imagine a stream going where you want it to. If it tries to go where it doesn't belong, build a mental dam to redirect it. Please, try again."

Camdus put the ring back on. The tsunami surge almost overwhelmed him, but he did as he was told. It was a river not a stream, but he was able to control it. He looked up when he realized what had happened. "I have control. What now?"

Vandalen replied without hesitation, "Summon my ring to me. It will come no matter where it is; it will come."

"How do I summon it? Is there a special word or gesture?" Vandalen smiled again, easier this time. "Just think of me, my ring, and me with my ring on my finger."

Camdus was stunned at the simplicity of it, "That's all?"

"Yes. That's all. Now, please summon my ring. We will need them both if we're to overcome Elsnor."

Camdus stepped away a bit to calm his jangling nerves. He took a deep breath and did as he was asked. Within a few moments, he heard Vandalen draw a quick breath. Turning, he saw the ring, slimy with river moss, sitting on Vandalen's right index finger. Camdus blinked in disbelief. He had not truly thought this would work, but now the possibilities were endless. Vandalen looked up from his ring and recognized the expression on the younger man's face. "Commander, do not let the ring take control of you. It is very tempting, especially after your first success with it. But you are stronger; you are better; you have purpose." As he spoke, he saw the struggle Camdus was fighting with the ring, but Vandalen knew Camdus had to fight this one alone.

In a few moments, Camdus spoke, beads of sweat sliding down his temples. "I understand now what you've been saying. This is not a thing I desire, but I know I have to use it for good. I'm okay now; the ring will not control me again. Now, we have to get back to Q'Door Hold. Things are just about to get interesting."

Vandalen nodded, though he would not have chosen the word 'interesting.' He followed Camdus back to Seelah's sitting room where they found the others deep in conversation.

"Seelah," Camdus greeted their host, "it is time for us to be about our business. Thank you for your help. If all goes well, we'll see you again. Pray for us."

Seelah said, with a resolved tone, "May God be with you. Elani and I will be waiting." Elani looked from her father to Slogar. No words were necessary; as always, her look said it all.

Vandalen stepped forth and gave his daughter an unexpected hug. "I'll be back in no time, Princess," he whispered in her ear. The endearment sent both joy and sadness straight as an arrow piercing her heart.

She clung to him a moment. "I will be waiting, Father."

Rax appeared at the Commander's summons. With a brief review of their strategy, Camdus asked Rax to take him and Vandalen back to Q'Door Hold. Slogar spoke up, "What about me, Cam? I can be of some use to you. Shouldn't I go also?" Cam had intended to leave Slogar here, but thought perhaps Slo was right. "All right, then. Rax please take Vandalen and me to Q'Door Hold; then come back for the doctor." Rax complied; in a few minutes he was back to fetch Slogar.

The Battle for Q'Door Hold

Rax had orders to find the Commander, wherever he was, no matter what. Slogar knew this, but had not thought much about it until the very moment they popped back into Q'Door Hold. Cam and Vandalen were back to back, outnumbered three to one by tall, helmeted Q'Aron soldiers. The appearance of the two interlopers threw the Q'Arons off balance for a split second. That was all Vandalen and Camdus needed. Vandalen yelled, "Now, Commander!"

Camdus knew what he had to do – he pictured the enemy overcome. He felt the power coursing through his body. The urge to let it run wild was strong, but he knew that he had to control it. He didn't want to kill, only to disarm and disable. Weapons flew from his combatants' hands, as they writhed in agony and fell to the floor. Vandalen's foes fared no better. Quickly, Camdus and Vandalen bound, gagged, and hid the now unconscious men. "Rax, get the doctor to the rest of the group. Go now!" Camdus shouted the order as he and Vandalen turned to face another onslaught. When the Q'Aron soldiers reached the center of the passageway, Camdus released the captives. The stunned Q'Arons screamed with pain and panic as they were slammed by their comrades who fell, bound and unconscious, from the ceiling. In haste, that had been the only place Camdus could think of to hide them.

Vandalen was amused, "Nicely done, Commander. But we've got to get this scum out of here. And we don't want them coming back. Any ideas?"

Rax popped at that moment. "Where would you like me to take them, Commander?"

Only Vandalen was surprised; Cam was used to Rax showing up when he needed him. To Rax he said, "Take them to Dartal; to Vandalen's cell." Four pops later, and the deed was done. Camdus thanked Rax, and instructed him to take a break. Cam was sure that it had been too long since Rax last ate; he needed his strength now more than ever.

Camdus and Vandalen were the only ones left in the passageway, but they knew they had to get to the rest of the group. Instead of summoning Rax, he led Vandalen to the end of the passageway and then down a level. There, right where he left them, were the rest of his men. Rax was sitting on the floor, eating jerky and drinking tredon milk. Clearly, he was enjoying his break.

Camdus filled them in on their skirmish upstairs. Then he asked Grunden for an update.

"First, thanks for the cloaking device. It works great. We were able to use it to cloak our location, but we also used it to send out scouts to see what else was here." He saw the disapproval registering on the Commander's face, so followed with, "I knew it would be risky, but we discussed our situation; to be practical, we couldn't just sit around and wait for your return, Commander." Camdus begrudgingly nodded.

Grunden continued. "Not long after you left, Ramar and I went on a scouting run to the upper level. We found a hidden stairway in the rear northern corner. Since most of the activity is usually to the south and east, we decided that would be our safest route. The journey revealed nothing until we got to the top. The entire floor was dark with only an eerie yellowish glow to light our way. When we rounded a corner, we heard something. We knew we were cloaked, but still solid, so we hugged the wall as close as we could. We saw a man carefully making his way along the hallway. He was so covered in blood and sand, he hardly looked human. We turned and followed him. He wound his way back the way we had come, but took a left into a minor corridor which ended outside a door secured by two burly guards. They told him to halt, but he charged them. He dodged a blast from one of the weapons, but was in the cross-hairs of the other's. I sent a stun blast to stop the guard from killing the man. He didn't see us, but knew he'd had help. He sprinted off on down the corridor and disappeared. With the one guard down, the other one struggled to lift his comrade, while keeping his weapon pointed in no particular direction. I stunned him, too, for we needed to see what was in that room. We knew we didn't have much time, but we carefully cracked the door and looked in. Elsnor was sitting alone, his back to us. Yet he spoke. 'Who's there?' We closed the door as quietly as we could and ran like mad in the same direction as the injured man. We've been back here ever since."

Camdus had listened closely to this recounting of Grunden's excursion. "So you know where Elsnor is?"

"Yes, Commander, we do," Grunden told Camdus, adding, "but if he knew we were there while we were cloaked and not even in the room, I don't see how we're going to be able to take him."

Ramar echoed this sentiment, "Elsnor has powers unlike anything we've ever seen. He looks like he's this weak old man, but everyone's afraid of him. And if I'm guessing right, the injured man was going to pay him a retribution visit. It sure didn't look like a social call."

Vandalen had been listening intently. "I know you said the man was covered in blood and dirt, but was there anything unique about him; anything at all?"

Ramar tried to remember. "He was tall, with long hair that was either gray or looked gray because it was full of sand — I couldn't tell. His clothes were black, but there was no emblem or mark on them."

"Gentlemen," Vandalen said solemnly, "I believe that man is my son, Serin. We need to find him; he needs our help."

Camdus had no intention of helping the mercenary and said so. "Vandalen, we need your help, but not if it means we have to bring your son into our midst. He's not the good son you remember."

Vandalen stood his ground, "Maybe so, but I am the good father whom I believe he will remember. If what you've told me about him is true, how could he have let himself get into this pitiful shape? If for no other reason, we need to find out who or what injured him, and how he survived the attack. Our own lives may depend on …."

Vandalen was interrupted by angry, desperate cries of one of the beasts. They knew that the beast could smell them, whether they were cloaked or not. The sound was getting closer by the second.

Camdus rallied his group with a battle cry that would have shaken the rafters if there'd been any. "Grunden, Stadar. Take your men to the service room to our left. Vandalen, go with them. The rest of you, come with me." He sprinted down the far hallway, his soldiers close on his heels.

He hoped that they would be able to trap the beast between them and destroy it. Before they had reached their assigned spot, the beast appeared. Its eyes glowed like the coals deep in the furnace belly; a mix of blood and saliva slopped out of its mouth. Without warning, it sprang toward the last man in Grunden's party. The soldier, trapped beneath the great hulk, blasted the beast with his nucleo. The great beast howled in pain, but renewed its attack. With one massive front paw, it smashed the soldier's skull, the contents splattering across the floor and up the wall. It then took the lifeless soldier in its vise-like jaws and slung him like he was nothing more than a rag. He stood on his hind legs, pawing the air as if challenging the men to battle.

Grunden recognized the soldier, a fresh recruit with a wife and small baby at home. Rage as he never known before flowed through him. He stepped out, screaming at the beast, "Come on, you coward! What? You can only take men whose backs are turned? Try me, you sorry piece of ....," his words were drowned by all the commotion in the corridor.

By now both Camdus and Vandalen had stepped into view, one slightly in front and to the left of the beast, the other directly to its right. "Grunden, get down!" Cam ordered. Grunden instantly obeyed; the beast was hit by double jolts of lightning – one silver, the other purple. The beast tried to extract itself from the current flowing through its body, but was no match. It fell, writhing on the floor. Cam and Vandalen lowered their right hands, stopping the voltage. Before their astonished eyes, the beast began to change form.

Ram strode over and looked down at the man who now lay where the beast had been and said to no one in particular,

"Lt. T'Aron. I should have known. Why else would he have been attracted to Li'Let." That solved one of the mysteries of Q'Door Hold.

Camdus knew that they only had seconds before more Q'Aron guards arrived for they could hear them approaching. They had to find Elsnor before the guards found them and engaged them in a fight. Any delay and Elsnor would escape. Cam spoke to Grunden, "Take us to Elsnor."

Grunden complied, activating the cloaking device as he took the lead. Once on the top level, they followed Grunden to the double doors. Those closest could hear voices.

"... Not this time, old man. Now it's my turn. You're not so arrogant without your ring, are you, Elsnor?" Vandalen recognized the voice. "Serin," he whispered to Camdus, "let me go in. We need Elsnor alive so we can find out how much he knows, if nothing else."

Camdus knew Vandalen was right, but he still didn't like the idea. "Go, but be careful."

Vandalen slipped into the room unnoticed by either of the men. Two Q'Aron guards were lying on the floor, their yellow blood pooling beside them. Serin was standing over Elsnor, his right hand on the old man's throat; the primitive weapon, an ancient dagger, held in his left hand was pressing against Elsnor's chest. Vandalen spoke evenly and calmly. "Son, don't do this thing. This is not who you are."

Serin whipped his head around to see his father without moving his hands. "You don't know who I am. How could you? Typical 'Father' mentality: Always take the other man's side; never stand up for you own." Elsnor's face was turning scarlet, the fight leaving him.

"Serin, we need Elsnor. He has information we need. Let him up – please." Elsnor felt the pressure on his neck slacken, but the point of the knife was still firmly planted at his chest. He started to speak, but thought better of it. He knew the slightest wrong word from him could precipitate his demise.

"Son, please. We need you, too. I need you. I've found your sister; actually, she found me. But she's safe." Vandalen wanted his son to respond through free will, not by any other force. He could see that the mention of Elani had struck a chord. Serin stepped back, jerking Elsnor to his feet as he came.

Serin, always quick to assess situations, looked at Vandalen. 'Father,' he thought, 'where were you when I needed you?' But he put no voice to these thoughts; this was not the time. Instead he stated, "I assume you are not alone, Father."

"Correct," Vandalen answered. "I believe the Commander will find this the perfect place for our headquarters." He strode to the door and summoned the others, who quickly and remarkably quietly entered the chamber. Elsnor had yet to recognize Vandalen, who had moved silently to one of the large windows. He stood with his back to the room.

Camdus posted guards at the doors; then he turned his attention to their captive. Elsnor eyed Cam's ring curiously. Vandalen still stood staring out into the dusk's dim light, but listened intently. Serin was in no mood for ancient Geneva Convention civility; he shoved Elsnor back into the chair – hard – keeping his knife at the ready. "Go ahead, old man. Just give me an excuse," he snarled. Camdus looked at him sharply. Though Serin had no scruples, Camdus knew he would not finish Elsnor – at least not yet. Cam pulled a chair up directly in front of Elsnor.

"You're going to tell us what we want to know, Elsnor. And you get to decide how you want to do it – one way you get the pleasure of an Empire Tribunal; or the other way, your last words will be to tell us where to send your remains. Like I said, you decide. But know this: what little patience I had has been gone for a very long time. Now, Elsnor, who are you working for? The Q'Arons, or yourself? Or is it some other group entirely?" Elsnor tried to muster his arrogant smile, but the swollen, bloody, mouth and missing teeth made it impossible.

Elsnor's bravado did the talking, "Do your worst. You can't hurt me." Camdus scoffed at this absurdity. "Sure we can, Elsnor. We haven't even started yet. But if you're waiting on your beasts or your guards to rescue you, you can forget it. We've met them; they won't be back. Now, let's start again. Who are you working for?"

Elsnor sat silently, staring ahead, clearly trying to see a way to turn this situation to his advantage. Cam sat patiently, absentmindedly stroking his ring. He felt the power coursing through him. He reminded himself of Vandalen's warnings and channeled his thoughts to his mental river.

Vandalen turned now from the window and faced Elsnor. At first, Elsnor didn't notice him, his eyes still on Cam's ring. When he looked up, he was looking straight into Vandalen's eyes. There was no mistaking his identity. The knowledge that the great wizard Vandalen was standing so close to him, with the ring he himself had seen thrown into the Jevishal neatly seated on his right index finger helped bring Elsnor around to a much more cooperative frame of mind.

"How did you....?"

"How did I get out of that hell hole on Dartal – the one you made sure I was sent to? Elsnor, you would never understand the power that freed me." Vandalen's cool voice chilled the room. Camdus had been sitting there watching this exchange impatiently.

Vandalen sensed that now was not the time to exact revenge; indeed, he knew there was never a good time, but one day....

"Commander, I believe our prisoner is ready to cooperate now," he said as he stepped back, with a sweeping gesture with his hand, inviting Camdus to continue.

"Who are you working for?"

Elsnor knew there was no alternative to truth. He answered, "Weilz."

Camdus pressed, "Weilz. What was really in it for him, other than moving up from second to first?"

Elsnor nodded, "It was not about power or wealth. It was revenge. Jarlod seduced Weilz' youngest daughter, I've forgotten her name, before she had reached her fifteenth year. He used his friendship with Jarlod and her mother to get to the girl, and then began inviting her to visit his own daughter. His depravity sickens even me, though I admit to fancying younger women. I would never stoop into that cesspool. Jarlod offered Weilz his current position in the Empire to appease him. When Weilz accepted, Jarlod thought all was well. In his own self-absorbed world, he could now see himself as the beneficent friend, not the perverted molester he truly was — and is. He never asked about the girl; he didn't want to know the wreckage of her gentle spirit and childish mind he'd left behind."

Vandalen and Camdus had listened intently. "So what enticement did he use to get your cooperation?"

Elsnor answered simply, "He offered me my own world, complete with everything I would need to have everything I've ever wanted."

"Which world?" Camdus demanded.

"Boldoon."

Grunden stepped forward, glowering down at their captive, "Creedor has a better chance of its demon winds calming forever than you taking my world, Elsnor. At least, not if I have anything to do with it."

Camdus spoke quietly to Grunden, "Enough, Mr. Grunden. Elsnor is full of . . . hot air. If he believes that Weilz would ever give him his own world, then he will find he was sadly deceived." To Elsnor he said, "Where are the Q'Aron leaders who are in Q'Door Hold?"

Elsnor managed a triumphant look despite his now discolored as well as swollen face, "They're gone. And they have all the trizactl they need to complete the weapons they will use to finish you off." He laughed bitterly, not for the

Q'Arons' victory, but at his own defeat. Camdus was sick of him; he stunned him into unconsciousness.

"That'll take care of him for a while," was all he said before addressing more pressing needs.

Cam realized that he had two injured men to contend with: Serin and Elsnor. "Rax," he said aloud. The soft pop was followed by Rax who, judging by the crumbs on his uniform, must have been eating when summoned.

"Yes, Commander?" Rax responded.

"Please bring Dr. Slogar to us. Tell him he has two patients waiting."

When Rax returned, Slogar had his small bag with him, eager to assist. He surveyed the situation, and decided that Serin, though full of fight, had the more pressing wounds.

"Mr. Serin, if I may...." Serin had not realized the extent of his injuries – he'd been running on pure adrenaline. Seating himself at one end of the long conference table beside the doctor, he allowed Slogar to examine his wounds.

"What happened to you, Mr. Serin?"

Serin snarled, "Does it matter? Just patch me up."

Slogar quickly responded, "It matters. If I know what made the wounds, then I can know better how to treat them."

Serin saw the logic. "These gouges here," he said pointing to the gaping wound in his side and the minor gouges on his arms and legs, "were made by the beast. The rest of them were made by some bush I tried to hide in. Damned thing tried to eat me!"

Slogar cleansed the wounds and applied an antiseptic ointment. He then pulled a needle and vial out of his bag to draw blood. Serin's objection was plain when they skittered across the polished steel floor after he knocked them from the doctor's hand.

"Now, Mr. Serin, please. My supplies are limited. We can't be wasting them."

"You're not sticking me with a needle. I've been stabbed enough!" Serin was adamant. But Slogar was just as insistent.

"I have to know if you've been infected with a disease, specifically the one killing Creedorians by the thousands. Now will you allow me to do my job?"

Serin stuck his arm out and endured the blood drawing, which to him was no more than an insect sting – as long as he looked away. Once Slogar had collected enough, he turned to Camdus and asked, "Can you get me back to Seelah? I need her to help me with this analysis." He handed a small jar to Camdus, "Here's some ointment for your prisoner."

Camdus took the ointment, though he thought it a waste, but he handed it to Rax and asked him to take Elsnor to Dartal to join his cronies. He then allowed the doctor to return to Seelah. In a moment, Rax and Slogar popped out once again.

When Rax got back, Camdus called together all his men to assess their strength and plan their strategy. He surveyed what was left of the group: Serin was banged up, but otherwise okay. Stadar, Grunden, and Ramar had formed a team that worked pretty well together. Rax was fearless and completely loyal, as was his nature. That left Vandalen and himself. He now knew that their power could be used together to overcome some fierce opponents. But he also knew there were dangers in using the power. Yet at this stage they had to go full out if they were to prevail.

"Gentlemen, please sit," Camdus indicated the chairs around the conference table. He seated himself at the head of the table. "When is the last time anyone saw Q'Arons?"

Stadar said, "I haven't seen any since we overpowered Elsnor and his bodyguards. That's been several hours ago."

"That's right, Commander," Ramar added, "and I think that tells us we need to get to the mines now. We can't stay up here. Remember what Elsnor said? The Q'Arons already have what they need and are ready to ship out with it."

"What he said was they're already gone. If that's so, we have a bigger problem. But you are right in one thing: we've got to get to the mines." Camdus said thoughtfully.

"Commander," Grunden interjected, "have any ships responded to our distress call yet?"

Camdus didn't want to answer this particular question; it would be too disheartening. But he knew he owed the men the truth. "No, and I don't expect we will. But what we lack in numbers we make up for in skill and power. We've just got to breach the Hold's docking station. And we need to do it now. Who knows how to get into that part of the enclave?"

Stadar spoke up, "I do, Commander. When I first got here, I worked in the mines. The docking station's at the base level on the eastern side of the mine. I'm pretty sure I can find it again. The closer we get, the hotter it is. There's a shaft off the transport tube that goes directly into heart of the mine, but out of the main traffic."

Vandalen had been listening quietly. Now he said, "That's fine, but what are we going to do when we get there?" Camdus understood Vandalen's impatience.

The Commander barked orders, "Grunden and Stadar, disable the transport pods, if they're still here. Rax, I want you and Ramar to neutralize their communicators. Serin, you're with me and Vandalen. Everyone be on your guard; if they get in your way, do what you have to do. But try to take them alive; we'll want to interrogate them later. Stadar, take the lead." With that they left the relative safety of the conference room in the abandoned tower and headed down, down into the hot belly of the planet.

Seelah sends for Serin

Once back in Silden, Slogar had no time to settle in. He briefed Seelah and they went straight to her lab.

"Simon, please give me the sample," Seelah was seated on a tall stool in front of a small contraption that looked like an old compact disc player from Earth's 1990's. She gingerly opened the vial and extracted a tiny dot of Serin's blood. She then placed the sample in the machine. While it whirred softly processing the sample, Seelah took a moment to talk to the doctor.

"What happened on Creedor, Simon? You look like you've been through forty hells."

Slogar, though surprised by her language, answered her as best he could. "We captured Elsnor, but not without the loss of some of our soldiers. Vandalen and Camdus killed one of the beasts, who turned out to be a changeling. It just got crazier from there. Serin was attacked by the beast, and by, according to him mind you, a bush. So I've brought his blood here for analysis to see if he's got the disease that's killing the folks on Creedor. That's pretty much it."

Seelah didn't say anything for a bit, but then she asked, "A bush? Are you sure he said 'a bush,' Simon? Bushes generally don't attack."

Slogar got the distinct impression that the Elder Woman was about make light of what he had told her, and frankly, he was in no mood for levity.

"I'm quite sure he said a bush tried to eat him. I know how that must sound, but Creedor is not your ordinary world.

Really strange things are happening there, so if he said it was a bush, then I believe him."

Seelah started to say something, but the results were back on the blood sample. "Well, I have good news and bad news, as the saying goes. Serin has contracted a disease and it's one that I think we can cure. The bad news is we don't have enough blood to culture an antidote."

"Do you think Serin has the disease we've been looking for?"

"I do. And your guess was right. He has rabies, but it's a new strain. Do you know how long ago he was bitten?"

"Two days ago, I think. If he has rabies, we have to treat him or he'll die but not before infecting the men he's with." He thought a minute, and then added, "Seelah, I think the strain is not a natural mutation. I think it's been engineered. Can you can find an antidote if that's the case?"

Seelah's reply was not the one he wanted to hear, "Simon, I probably can, though it's very unlikely that it will be in time. However if we can get Serin here, then I think we'll at least have a chance. Perhaps you'd better get back to the Commander and see if he can persuade Serin to leave the fray for a bit."

Slogar said, "I'll try but there's no guarantee. Camdus can't order him to do anything. Maybe Vandalen can."

"I don't think Vandalen can sway Serin to do anything either, Simon. Their relationship is too broken. But Elani could."

Slogar nearly roared, "No! I won't have Elani going to Q'Door Hold, Seelah. It's just too dangerous."

"What's too dangerous?" Elani asked. She came in on the end of the conversation. Slogar and Seelah were facing each other, each ready to make a case for Elani either going or staying.

"Elani, we need to get your brother back here as quickly as possible. He's been infected with a very serious disease. If he's to survive, I need him here so that I can try to find an antidote."

Elani spoke without hesitation, "Of course. Where is he? Can Rax take me to him?" Slogar blurted out his objections; his genuine concern for her was evident in his every word.

"No, Elani. Please don't go. Your brother is at Q'Door Hold which is at this very moment in the middle of a siege. It's far too risky." He knew he was wasting his breath this time just like when he tried to keep her out of Dartal. 'Damn,' he thought, 'this is one stubborn woman.' Any other time, he'd find that quality somewhat challenging, but interesting, but not this time. All he could do was pray for her safety for he knew come what may, she would go to her brother.

"Simon," Elani spoke softly, "I will be back. And Serin will be with me. You and Seelah get everything ready. We'll be back before you know it."

Simon knew when he'd lost, so he contacted Camdus.

"Cam, Seelah needs Serin back here ASAP. He has rabies, possibly a genetically engineered strain. We have to have him here to run more tests and then to formulate an antidote. Elani wants to go to Q'Door Hold to fetch him. Can Rax accommodate?"

Cam's voice over the communicator was barely audible there was so much static. "Rax is t - - d up right h- - - at the mome- - - dis - - ing commu- - -tors and - - -spods." The communication crackled one last time and then fell completely silent. Slogar knew that things were far worse than they had been when he left. He only hoped that Camdus had understood his request and would send Serin anyway.

Elani said nothing. She left the room returning in a few moments with a tray of thistle tea. This time it was spiked with mulled wine. Slogar gladly accepted the mug she offered him. They sat on the sofa by the fireplace, not speaking, sipping their hot tea. After a bit, they heard a soft pop. They rose and turned to see Rax returning with Serin, who had been wounded yet again. Rax laid his unconscious charge on the sofa.

Seelah immediately went to the injured man to examine his wounds, which were very serious. She asked Rax and Slogar to take him to her lab.

Once the men had placed Serin on the raised bed, Rax addressed Slogar.

"Doctor, the Commander wants you and the Elder Woman to be ready for more guests. Not all of them are human."

Simon asked, "What do you mean, not human? What's down there, Rax?"

Rax told Slogar, "They are changelings, Doctor. We found a nursery, abandoned by the Q'Arons. In it, there are half dozen immature changelings. Perhaps cute by your standards, but knowing what they grow into, not at all safe to be around. The Commander feels we have to save them, even though they grow into beasts."

"You mean Camdus intends to send six of those beasts here, to Silden? Has he lost his mind?!"

Rax nodded affirmatively, leaving Slogar to interpret which of his questions he was answering. He then departed quite as suddenly as he'd arrived.

Losing Serin was a serious blow to Camdus; he had proven to be a fearless warrior. The heat from the mines was stifling, making it difficult for the men to breathe. Vandalen and Grunden were behind one of the disabled transpods, battling a group of the hooded Q'Arons. Stad and Ram were pinned behind the transport tube, unable to do anything but fend off the attacking Q'Aron beasts. Had Camdus known what he was leading them into, he might have waited until he could convince Jarlod to send help. As for his own predicament, he had cornered two fairly young looking Q'Arons he was sure he could subdue. But as soon as he blasted them, they changed into raging beasts. Now it was he who was cornered. He imagined a protective barrier around him, but the beasts attacked it again and again. Camdus couldn't keep the shield up much longer, and in his last moment of desperation, he reached into the pouch for his father's last gift. He pulled the small red feather out of the bag and instinctively stroked it three times. The feather leapt from his hand, becoming a huge winged beast, part lizard, part bird. Its talons were the size of a man and razor sharp. It rose above the battle and roared. The beasts, startled by the new threat, screamed and ran, leaving their prey unharmed. The alarmed Q'Arons threw down their weapons and knelt in submission.

Vandalen and the rest of the unit walked across the body littered battleground that the Hold had become. With the exception of Serin's injuries, Camdus and his small band had come through it almost unscathed. Breathing a silent prayer of thanks, Camdus walked over to the kneeling figure that bore the most adornment on his uniform. Though Camdus was unfamiliar with Q'Aron military practices, he guessed this one might be an officer. The Reglon beast had come to rest atop the largest of the transpods and quietly observed what was going on below. Camdus knew that he would have no trouble as long as the beast was there. How long that might be, he had no way of knowing.

"Grunden, I want you to take Stadar and Ram and secure the enemy; bring them back to headquarters. Vandalen, please come with me."

Once the others were gone, Camdus spoke to Vandalen, gesturing toward the great beast still looking down at them. "What do you know about this beast?"

Vandalen was as shocked as the rest and said so. "How would I know? You're the one who brought it here. How did you do that anyway?"

Camdus knew he needed his father's help. "I don't know, but I'm going to find out. You go ahead and help with the prisoners. I'll be up shortly."

Vandalen gave Camdus a quizzical look, but with one glance up at the huge beast, he was on his way.

Camdus leaned against the wall and contacted his father, all the while watching his companion who was now preening its feathers. When Willem answered, Camdus got straight to the point.

"Dad, you know the package you gave me before I left for the Academy? I've found the first two items extremely helpful. By the way, we need to talk about the whole wizard thing. But the third — the feather, I'm not sure what to do with the animal it has become."

Willem laughed heartily, "You must mean Sorbeau, my old friend and protector."Willem then sobered instantly, "So this means you found yourself with no other options. Son, are you all right?"

Camdus quickly filled his father in on what had happened since they last spoke; then asked, "Dad, do you think you and Tomer can join us here in Q'Door Hold? We can use men with your experience to help us with the interrogations - and with Sorbeau." Willem agreed to contactTomer and then get back to him.

Within an hour, Camdus got a call from Willem. He let Cam know that he and Tomer were ready to go Q'Door Hold. Cam gladly dispatched Rax to bring his father and Tomer to them.

Slogar and Seelah's Discovery

When Serin opened his eyes, he was greeted by the sight of his sister seated by his bedside. He thought she was napping, and couldn't help himself.

"Well, Sis, I guess I know how much you've worried about me. Sleeping like a baby, and right here by my bed no less." Though he was teasing her, Elani responded seriously.

"I was praying, Brother, not napping." Elani then softened her voice, and said to Serin, "Slogar and Seelah gave up hope for your recovery. But I knew with all my being that you would wake up. And I am thankful I was right, even if you did wake only to aggravate your sister."

Duly chastened, Serin asked, "How long have I been here? The last thing I remember is being dragged by one of the beasts by my ankle. It felt as if my leg was about to be ripped off, the pain was so bad." Elani knew she had to tell him, but was unsure as to how. She started, "Serin, Slogar and Seelah tried; I mean to say they really did everything they could to ...., but everything was so mangled, they couldn't."

Thoroughly confused, Serin asked his sister, "What are you saying? Just say it, Elani. They tried to do what?" But before she could answer, he looked down and realized that his left leg was missing from just below knee down. He let out a roar of anguish. Elani burst into tears, her sorrow for her brother flooding down her face.

Seelah and Slogar heard the commotion and hurried into Serin's room. He glared at them. "What have you done to me? What in God's name have you done?"

Seelah was prepared for this, but it was not easy. "Serin, to save your life, we took your leg. A good trade, we thought, though I can see that you do not agree."

"You took my leg. You took my leg. How could you? I didn't even get a say in it. What did you expect me to say? 'Thanks for saving my life, and, oh by the way, it's okay that I'm crippled.' Well, I can't be that magnanimous. You didn't save my life, you took it. How am I supposed to live now?"

Seelah waited until he was finished, then she said, "Serin, do you remember being attacked by a bush?"

Serin was in no mood to play stupid guessing games. "Hell yes, I remember being attacked by a bush. What's that got to do with anything?"

Slogar took over, "Everything. The bush you were attacked by is known as a miracle bush. It left its DNA in your blood, and from it we have formulated a cure for the disease that is ravaging Creedor. Not only that, if our research is correct, it is possible that your missing leg may – MAY, not will, for we can't be sure – regenerate in time. You'll just have to wait and see."

Serin lay back exhausted by trying to digest all this information at once. He did get that his blood had been instrumental in finding the cure to the disease killing Creedorians. And his leg might grow back! That's where it became too much. He looked at the three standing by his bedside, closed his eyes, and for the first time since he was a young boy, he began to pray. He drifted off to sleep, not knowing what the rest of his life would be, but knowing one thing for sure – it would not be the same as it had been.

Seelah checked to make sure Serin's vital signs were good; then she left Slogar with Elani, who showed no signs of leaving her brother's side.

"Elani," Slogar began gently, "you've been here since yesterday. You need to eat and to rest. Please come with me; I'll prepare you a meal, meager though it may be, but nourishing all the same. Serin is going to be fine. While he's resting, you should, too." Elani looked into Simon's eyes and read his concern for her. She had perhaps been selfish, she thought. "All right, Simon, but let me help you. We make a pretty good team at catching supper, so we should make a good team preparing it. Besides I find cooking a very cathartic activity." He held out his hand to her, which she took gladly. They went to Elani's garden to gather a few fresh vegetables and herbs before returning to cook. Simon could feel her spirit lifting.

As she bent to pick fresh dill, he said so softly she almost didn't hear, "Elani, marry me."

Elani dropped the dill and stood to face him. "You know that we would never have children, Simon."

"Elani, I want to spend what's left of my life with you, if you'll have me. I'm too set in my ways for children anyway, though if we did by some miracle have them, then that would be fine — as long as they took after you."

Elani picked up the dill, stood up straight, and gave him the answer he'd longed to hear. Simon Slogar could not believe his good fortune, but intended to make every day with Elani as full as possible. With God's help, he would be the husband Elani deserved.

Rax popped back into the conference room with two complete strangers. Camdus was taken aback, but knew that Rax didn't make mistakes. He always brought back who or what he'd been sent to retrieve. He'd just have to trust that these men were in some way connected to his father and Tomer. Perhaps they'd been sent by him. Still baffled, he decided not to let the others know his doubts.

"Commander, allow me to introduce myself, Zachary Radfield, at your service. And let me introduce my colleague, Lenwood Styles. How may we be of assistance?" Cam recognized his father's voice, if not his appearance. He welcomed them with a brief handshake, followed by his request, "Mr. Radfield, I understand that you speak fluent Q'Aron and are equally familiar with their customs. Is that correct?"

"Quite right, Commander. Lenwood and I are both experts in both these areas. That's why I asked him to join me. I hope you don't mind."

Cam found this whole cloak and dagger routine disturbing, but knew his father had reasons for everything he did.

"Well then, Gentlemen. We should get started. I need to find out everything about this facility, its purpose, and how much of their mission has been accomplished.

"Stadar, please bring in the officer." In a few minutes, Zachary and Lenwood were conversing with the Q'Aron officer. Though Cam spoke some Q'Aronese, he would have to rely on his father and Tomer to get to the truth, if that was possible.

Willem spoke to the man first; then Tomer took over. The interrogation seemed to be going nowhere until Willem took a small item from his pocket. It looked like a seven pointed star carved from an unusual substance that gave off an orange pulsing glow. As soon as the officer, whose name Tomer had learned was T'Engler, saw the object yellow sweat began to bead on his forehead, his words became calmer and flowed more easily. After another fifteen minutes, T'Engler's eyes rolled back in his head and he slumped in his chair, passed out cold. Camdus stepped into the room with the trio.

"What happened? Is he dead?" Cam asked, fearing the worst.

"No, he just couldn't take any more exposure to the Q'Aron Sacred Star. They are physically unable to lie in its presence. I tried to get him to talk without it, because exposure can be lethal, but he wouldn't budge. However, I think we've learned much of what you need to know. Thankfully your prisoner has a strong constitution. He'll be out for quite some time, but he will revive."

"That's a relief. Now tell me what he said," Camdus pressed.

"The Q'Arons have been here for about two years, though the facility itself was finished only a few weeks ago. Their mine is directly below Q'Door Hold, which is why the lower levels are so hot. Trizactl mining generates incredible amounts of energy, which manifests as heat. They were sent here by the Q'Aron Emperor Hellritch himself to steal what they needed to complete their power plants first and then to build a store of hugely lethal weapons. Just one of them can tear a chunk out of a planet large enough to knock it out of orbit, effectively destroying all life on it. But the destruction won't be sudden, which would be kind, if destruction can ever be described as such. As the planet moves farther and farther from its sols, its inhabitants will begin to die from hunger, exposure, and insanity." When Willem paused, Tomer took up the story.

"They have taken twenty thousand tons of trizactl from this mine. It is on its way back to the Q'Aron Empire. If it is allowed to arrive, it is only a matter of time before our own Empire will be destroyed, one planet at a time."

"But why," Camdus asked, "why destroy us? We've co-existed for eons, peacefully before Jarlod ticked them off. Why now? What can they possibly expect to gain for our demise?"

Tomer answered, matter-of-factly, "To answer why, it's because they can. You see, to the Q'Arons, nothing outside their realm is sacred. Yet they have a religion; they worship the Sacred Star. Its seven points, they believe, represent their victory over seven galaxies. Ours is the first. At least, that is what T'Engler told us; and I believe him. There would have been no need to steal our trizactl if they already had the weapons they needed. Unfortunately, that's not the only reason they built this facility."

Camdus could think of nothing worse, but asked anyway. "What other reason?"

"They have been breeding changelings. Their plan for them was to set them loose in their own worlds to keep their populace in check. Population control, maybe; keeping the citizens powerless, for sure."

"You said their plan 'was' to set the changelings loose. What happened to the plan? Did they succeed?" Camdus asked.

Willem set his mind at ease, "The plan failed miserably. The changelings were too hard to control, so they aborted that part of the mission."

"The nursery. There are infant changelings in the nursery on one of the lower levels. I think we need to take them to Seelah to see if she can help them."

Up until this point, Ramar had stood in one corner, quietly taking in every detail. But now he spoke up.

"Commander, are you serious? Have you forgotten what these things are capable of when they are fully mature? I say we destroy them here and now."

Vandalen stood by Cam. "No, we can't kill the young changelings. They will grow into whatever they are raised to become. Here, they were brought up to be heartless murderers. With a different environment and kinder handling, they can become gentle beings who may at some point in the future return the kindness with loyalty."

Ramar shook his head and walked out of the room. He had no choice but to acquiesce to his commander, but he sure as hell didn't have to like it. The best thing for him to now would be to get back to Mara to try to regain some sense of sanity in his life.

Camdus followed him out, "Ramar. Listen, we're going to need a strong man to oversee Q'Door Hold. How would you feel about taking on that task?"

Ramar turned, astonished that the commander would make such an offer, especially now. "No, Sir. I want to start over with a new tredon herd, maybe in one of the valleys this time. I think Mara would like that better. Besides, I'm not a soldier like Stadar. Maybe he'd like a posting here."

Camdus had expected as much. Perhaps Grunden and Stadar would agree to work together to rebuild a Reglon presence on Creedor. He'd have to convince Jarlod of the wisdom of this. But there was the matter of Weilz. With the evidence Cam had of Weilz' treachery, he was fairly sure that Jarlod would handle him as harshly as Weilz had handled those who got in his way. He knew he would have to deal with Jarlod's wickedness sooner or later, but right now he had to tread very carefully with the Emperor.

Cam's communicator buzzed to life. A message was coming in from a Reglon warship that Jarlod had finally sent to help. He shook his head and let the ship's captain know what had happened and what he needed to wrap up the operation here.

Soon there were Reglon soldiers fanning out to search the entire Hold. Sorbeau was sent to take care of the adult changeling beasts that had escaped when he appeared. The young changelings were taken to Seelah. Camdus made sure the Q'Aron prisoners were taken to Vuthral to await military trial. Finally, with Q'Door Hold secured, Camdus and his troops along with his father and Tomer were transported back to his ship.

The antidote to the Creedorian disease had been dispensed by a small army of medics trained by Slogar and his assistants. Jarlod had hurriedly commissioned the Medic Corps to handle the medical issues on Creedor. Thankfully, the divided families had been reunited. Alone and bone tired, Camdus went back to his quarters, washed the filth of battle from his body, and tried to wash it from his mind. He was just settling into his chair for much needed rest when he was alerted to a visitor requesting entry. When the door softly closed behind her, Rayalla stood, unsure of what to say or if coming here was a huge mistake. Her heart was thudding in her chest. With all the courage she could muster, she whispered his name, half hoping he'd send her away. But Cam's own heart was pounding, for he could not accept that the only woman he'd ever cared for was standing right here, right now. He rose and embraced her. They talked until she read the tiredness in his eyes. After she left, he fell into the most peaceful sleep he'd had in a very long time.

But sometime, in the wee hours of the morning, Camdus awoke with the knowledge that the fight had only lulled. He had to stop the Q'Arons from completing their weapons. And he knew just who he was going to tap for the journey. With a bound out the door, he called his team together.

"Men, we have a mission."

Rax sat languidly beside the stream behind his home. He cherished this time away from battle, away from riding. He watched as his wife Evy and their children splashed each other in the shallow water. The massive meal Evy had prepared for them was just settling when he sensed the call. He strode into the water, fully clothed, and embraced his wife. She looked up at her husband; she knew. He kissed his daughter Zil and tousled his young son Kel's hair. A soft pop, and he was gone.

Made in the USA
Charleston, SC
18 September 2010